# A MELODY FOR MADELINE

# A MELODY FOR MADELINE

T. WENDY WILLIAMS

Gallien G5 Publishing

# Contents

To my parents:
Terry and Bobbie
inspirations behind my imagination

Cover Design: Candice Kilgore
Cover Photo: Mikhail Nilov
Author Photo: Kim Taylor

First Printing, 2022

# Other works by the Author

Mile High Confessions
Happily Never After
Lost in the Music

# One

Last night, August 18, 1987, I performed Robert Schumann's "Toccata in C Major, Op. 7" with the Los Angeles Philharmonic, one of the best philharmonic orchestras in the country. When I finished, the audience gave me a standing ovation, and that was the last thing I remember.

I went from feeling on top of the world to now feeling like the world is on top of me. I'm eight weeks pregnant. My daddy says I'm keeping it—abortion and adoption, not an option.

My daddy suggests I marry the father. Why? My daddy is a Methodist minister with an exceptionally large following. Having an unwed teenaged pregnant daughter isn't a good look for him. This isn't good for my image either. My future appeared promising. I'm supposed to be attending Juilliard next week, but that's not the case anymore. My daddy says I need to stay where I get emotional support. Home for me is Houston, Texas, but I don't want to go back, so I'll remain here in L.A. with my extended family and close to the father of my unborn child. Earlier today, I heard my conscious speak in a voice sounding like my deceased mother's. It said, *I am not ready to see my grandbaby.* Then I heard, *When the time comes, you'll be ready.*

No. I'm not.

Now everyone's deciding what's best for us. When I say *everyone*, I'm talking about my daddy, my aunt Mary, and the parents of the father—which technically makes them grandparents. What's weird? The father and I weren't in a relationship. JB is the best friend of my first cousin Caleb. They've been friends forever. They're on the same university basketball team; they're in the same fraternity. JB is like a play cousin who until this summer, I never looked at in any other way. The summers before, I'd see him hanging out playing basketball. Yes, I thought he was cute, but that was it. But this summer, he looked different. I can't explain it.

There were five of us together on the beach: me, my first cousins Cassandra and Caleb, JB, and their friend, Jake. We were all playing, then everyone left, and it was just JB and me. We were alone, swimming, and I remember we stopped and gazed into each other's eyes.

I was like, "What?"

He was like, "What?"

The strangest attraction washed over us like a tidal wave. I could tell he wanted to kiss me, but he didn't want to take it there, not then anyway. Later, I discovered we had something in common, a passion for the piano. I had years of formal lessons. He only took lessons for a brief time, but he could play the "William Tell Overture" as if he had been training for years. He impressed me with his interest in music, even classical music. He said I needed to "expand my musical ears." He introduced me to artists like Queen, George Duke, Sade, and yes, the World Class Wreckin' Cru. We enjoyed live music performances in venues we weren't old enough to get into. We spent hours writing, producing, and listening to music.

He has a worn-down black-and-white speckled, composition notebook with pages of lyrics written. He says all the songs are about me. I recall reading lyrics describing me: *angel face with sensuous curves, lips plump and juicy, honey butter skin with golden eyes that hypnotize.* I didn't know I had such an effect where he describes his knees weakening, eyes rolling in the back of his head, passion rising, body yearning, and a burning desire to have me.

Now we sit alone in my aunt Mary's dining room. My amber-colored eyes are a red, swollen mess from crying. The door opens, and Aunt Mary, my mother's oldest sister, appears.

"We're waiting," she says to us.

JB and I sigh collectively before we stand and follow her into the living area. Awaiting us are my daddy and JB's parents, James and Judy. James is tall and imposing. Judy is a petite Filipina who looks more like JB's sister than his mother. Their expressions are a combination of anger and hurt. Gilda, Daddy's assistant who also manages all my professional affairs, sits next to him, her chin rests on her knuckles. She doesn't say much when it comes to my personal matters. I've learned over the years that unless her opinions are asked, she keeps her thoughts to herself. What I love most about Gilda, she's a good listener, and she's effective at getting me work. She has upcoming performances scheduled for me. The question is will I keep them. By December, I will be six months pregnant and probably showing. Daddy says the optics are favorable if I'm married. As crazy as it sounds, if JB asks me to marry him, I think I would.

"I want a paternity test," James, JB's father, says.

I hear a gasp from Gilda, and I notice Aunt Mary and Judy frowning.

"Why?" Daddy asks.

"If JB's the father, I need to see it in writing," James answers.

"Fine. Get the test. My daughter is a young lady of integrity. She says he's the father; I take her word."

James, a former basketball star with the Los Angeles Lakers, says to JB, "I can't believe as much as I've schooled you, you still got caught up."

JB shrugs as he searches for words. "Things happen," he utters.

"This wasn't the plan, son. The plan was one, get through your junior year and win a championship. This pregnancy, it's a distraction," James says.

"But James, her father has spoken," Judy says. "Abortion and adoption are off the table."

"In this case, it's necessary. She's seventeen, and he's twenty. That's far too young to be dealing with this."

"Necessary?" Daddy questions. "Abortion? Necessary? I disagree with you only because I believe in Psalm 139, beginning with chapter thirteen: 'For God formed my inward parts and knit me together in my mother's womb—my frame was not hidden from God, when I was being made in secret, intricately wrought in the depths of the earth."

"Save your Bible-quoting scriptures for the church." While James talks, I notice Judy rubs his arm in a manner to calm him.

As Daddy and James exchange words, Aunt Mary sits quietly in her chair—only her eyes move. She was a child psychiatrist who gave up a thriving practice in Beverly Hills to open a youth center in one of the roughest neighborhoods in L.A. She's five-feet-four, just an inch taller than me, but her presence is enormous. Attentive most times, she blames herself for not being responsible enough or not keeping watch over me. I can't let her take on that burden. She was busy operating her youth center, never suspecting that I was behaving counter to her expectations.

"It's more than quoting scriptures. It's about aligning with God's Word," Daddy says.

"I don't read the Bible enough, but I know God forgives," James says. "In this situation, an abortion isn't wrong when it's the best choice."

Daddy sits quietly, shaking his head.

I don't like the idea of a paternity test. I mean I understand it, but it's just an ugly reminder of how crazy my summer was. There was one other person besides JB, but I'm positive he's not the father.

Just three months ago, I promised to be his girl, but something kept tugging at my heart. I wasn't into him like I thought. Less than two hours ago, while standing in Aunt Mary's foyer, I broke the news of my pregnancy to him, and just like that, I let him go and ran into JB's arms.

"Maddie and I can handle this," says JB who sits next to me on the edge of his chair. He's six-eight, amazingly handsome, with long, lean legs and big, strong hands that can palm a basketball and other round objects I won't mention. He's a star basketball player at his university. I've never been to any of his games, but I have been inside his bedroom. His walls are covered with basketball accolades, and he's on the covers of various sports magazines. He must be good if he's getting all that attention.

James closes his eyes and shakes his head. "Son, you can't."

"Why? You and Mom did it."

"I was two years into the league before I met your mother."

"Listen, I'll take a paternity test. Once you find out that *I am* the father, I'll do what I said I would: I'll declare myself eligible for the draft," he says then turns to me, "and somewhere find time for us to make it official. I want to be with you."

A warm, tingling sensation simmers inside causing the hairs on my arms to stand. My heartbeat escalates. I open my mouth to speak, but nothing comes out. My emotions are in a whirlwind, and I'm fighting to remain poised. James clasps his hands behind his head and releases a long, exasperated sigh.

"I can't believe this." He sounds disgusted.

"Aren't you always telling me to handle business like a man?" JB asks.

James is silent.

Daddy steps in. "James, we can't change what happened between our children, and we can't discard what's truly God's creation. As a minister of God's Word, my mission is to heed God's purpose. I don't question. I just know if it's from God, it must be good."

James is still silent. When Judy reaches to touch him, I notice he brushes her hand away. She quickly glances at JB for his reaction. JB sits up in his chair, eyeing his father. I'm feeling tension between them. I wouldn't want to see them get physical.

James begins, "They are not ready for this."

"I've counseled members of my church whose daughters terminated their pregnancies. The psychological toll it takes is insurmountable." Daddy turns to Aunt Mary. "Mary, you agree?"

Aunt Mary sits with arms folded and legs crossed. "It's a Catch-22," she says. "If the tables were turned, James, what if Maddie were your daughter? Eugene, what if JB were your son? Would you feel the same?"

"I honestly don't know," James answers.

Daddy ponders the question for a minute. "JB, if you were my son, I'd make sure you keep excelling in basketball while behind the scenes I'd guide you on what it takes to be a father and a husband."

James mumbles under his breath.

"I just met you today," Daddy says to JB, "and I can tell already that when you put your mind to something, you are diligent and dedicated."

"Thank you, sir. I appreciate that," JB replies.

I notice him glance at James for his reaction.

"To possess those traits, that's rare for someone your age," Daddy continues.

James scoffs in a way to suggest Daddy doesn't need to point that out. I get the sense we'll be at odds, even after he finds out JB's the father.

"I feel the need to pray," Daddy says to all of us. "There's a spirit of heaviness and uncertainty in this room. Let's gather and hold hands, please."

All of us except James gather in a circle. Daddy patiently waits for him. After a couple of seconds, James reluctantly joins us.

"All heads bowed, and all eyes closed, please." When Daddy begins a prayer with that line, most people follow suit. James clearly demonstrates he's not most people. "Father God, You knew about this day long before any of us in this room. And because You are all-knowing, we're coming to You asking You for Your guidance. Order our steps. Give us direction. Give us clarity. Give us peace. Give us more faith."

"While you're at it, give us some sanity," I hear James utter.

I open my eyes and see Daddy shaking his head, trying to remain calm. In a split second, my nausea returns, and I excuse myself and run down the hallway to the half bath. Falling to my knees, I bury my face in the toilet, and I wish I were numb—at least I wouldn't feel so much pain. All the food from earlier is swimming in the toilet water. Splashes of it hit me in the face as I erupt. I hear footsteps, and I recognize their cadence and then a familiar scent of leathery teakwood. I hear more footsteps.

I lift my face from the toilet seat and see JB. His eyes are worried and expressive.

"I'm okay," I assure him before flushing the toilet.

I notice Aunt Mary, Gilda, and Judy standing in the doorway.

"I'm okay. You all can leave now," I say to them.

"Would you like a ginger ale and a cool face towel?" Aunt Mary asks.

I nod, feeling fresh tears fall down my cheeks.

She leaves while Gilda and Judy remain.

"Maddie, you have me," Judy says.

Gilda takes her hand and squeezes it. It's amazing, they just met like three hours ago, and the news of my pregnancy has bonded them together like old lifelong friends. Gilda sighs, which makes me tear up more because I know what she's thinking, and I feel so bad for disappointing her. JB grabs a wad of tissue to hand me so I can dab at my swollen eyes.

"We'll leave you two alone," Gilda says before she and Judy walk away.

Moments later, I hear Aunt Mary's footsteps nearing, and she appears in the doorway with a glass of ginger ale and a damp face towel. We both thank her, and for a minute, there's an awkward silence in the air. I guess she's still coming to terms with our situation.

"If you need anything else, let me know," she says, and I hear her walk away.

I sip the ginger ale before resting my head on JB's shoulder. He pats my forehead and neck with the cold face towel, then I hear the sweetest voice singing:

*I know it's been a while*
*But I want to see you smile*
*Believe me, I feel your pain*
*It's falling like the rain*
*Promise me with a kiss*
*I only want one wish*
*I want to see you smile*
*I need to see you smile*

His singing voice is tenor. His tone is warm and free flowing; it's smooth and silky. I picture a million ripples in a vast sea when I hear it.

"Who sings that song?" I ask.

"What do you mean *who*? It's my song."

"You wrote that?"

"Not yet."

"You just made that up?"

"Yup."

"Wow." I look into his eyes, and I can't contain my excitement. I remember just how talented he is and when he's feeling vulnerable, how the words and melodies flow from him effortlessly.

"See, that's what I've been waiting on," he says, referring to my smile.

He has me smiling through my tears.

"This sounds super weird: I don't even know your birthday. How crazy is that?" he asks.

It's beyond crazy. We know of each other, but we really don't know each other, yet here we are, and in seven months, we'll be parents to a baby.

"It's February 14," I answer.

"I see I'll be working overtime."

"Why?"

"Your birthday and Valentine's Day. Can't celebrate one without the other."

"My parents always made sure I had a birthday cake and Valentine's Day cupcakes topped with strawberries and pink buttercream icing."

"Word." He nods.

"I had a birthday gift and a Valentine's Day gift."

"See, now you expect me to keep that tradition going, right?"

I notice he glances at my sterling silver necklace with the treble clef pendant. It wasn't a birthday or Valentine's Day gift, but a graduation gift from my cousin Caleb when I arrived in L.A. this summer.

"I was with Caleb when he picked this out," JB says.

I finger it, remembering the hurt on my cousin's face when he discovered JB and I had been together. The hurt grew to anger when I told him I was pregnant. The light catches the diamonds on my bracelet. This was a gift from my ex-boyfriend, Gregory Washington III. The eighteen-carat yellow-gold bracelet came with a tiny screwdriver. I was going to unfasten it and give it back to him when we broke up, but he claimed he lost the screwdriver. I feel bad for the way things ended with us. Twenty-four hours ago, we were together in my hotel suite, getting ready for my performance. Now he's probably somewhere hating and cursing the day he met me.

"What's your favorite song?" JB's random question interrupts my thoughts.

I think of classical music. It's the music my mother loved and she taught me to love. "I guess it would have to be Chopin's "Prelude in E minor." I'll play it for you when I get the chance. By the way, I don't think your father likes me."

"He'll come around."

"He won't. To him, I'll always be *that girl.*"

JB says, "Like your daddy said, if this is God's plan, then it has to be good."

I keep that thought in mind as the evening progresses.

"Let's talk about marriage," Daddy says once JB and I return to the living room.

"See, that's another thing," James begins. "You're in a rush to get them married. Am I the only one who has a problem with this?"

"I'll have to agree with James," Aunt Mary interjects. "Marriage is not the answer. We have a seventeen- and a twenty-year-old who barely know each other put in a life-changing situation. We've seen this time and time again. Shotgun marriages do not last."

"Mary," Daddy begins, "Madeline made a choice to have sex. Unprotected. Premarital sex. God is not pleased with that. I'm looking at this from a moral and spiritual perspective. Marriage is the right thing."

"If I didn't know better, I'd say you were making this all about you," James declares, "and how your church perceives you. If I were you, I'd tell them all to go to hell."

"Now, James," Judy says, tapping his arm.

"My son is a D1 athlete at the top of his game. He can't afford distractions."

The tone of James' voice echoes in the room. I look at Daddy, and I can tell all of this bothers him.

"What is the plan moving forward?" the psychiatrist in Aunt Mary asks.

"I'll say this," Daddy begins, "Maddie is having this baby. Maddie will keep her concert engagements, Maddie will stay connected to Juilliard, and I don't believe I'm being unreasonable when I say I'd like to see her married."

Everyone looks at James. "I've said what I had to say" is his response.

With that, he stands, signaling he's had enough. Daddy, who's only five-ten, stands and extends his hand.

"We can't move forward if we're constantly fighting," Daddy says.

"I'm doing whatever it takes to protect my son's interests."

As he, Judy, and JB prepare to leave, I feel like there's more still needed to be said, but instead I exchange pleasantries with Judy. My interaction with James is awkward. JB and I embrace.

"Call when you get a chance," he whispers.

It seems neither of us wants the evening to end.

# Two

It's a little after nine p.m., and my first cousin Cassandra slams the door to the Jack-and-Jill bathroom that connects our bedrooms. Minutes later, the toilet flushes then I hear water flow from the faucet. She usually opens the door and jumps on the foot of my bed, and we talk. Sometimes she grabs a brush, and as we talk, she brushes all eighteen inches of my hair, from root to ends. Right now, I expect the door to open any second, but it doesn't. I get up to check on her and can't turn the knob because it's locked.

"Cassandra." I tap lightly on her door.

The door opens slightly, and she appears. She's fair complected with keen features and unusually colored eyes—depending on her surroundings they appear a mixture of green and blue. When she's angry, the whites of her eyes are blazing, like they are now.

"How could you, Maddie?"

"Can we talk?"

She opens the door wide, and I find a spot on the edge of her bed to sit. She sits opposite me, and for a minute, we are quiet. We're both gathering our thoughts.

"Gregory stopped by Kyle's house after he left here."

Kyle is her boyfriend, plus he and my ex-boyfriend, Gregory are friends.

"What did he say?" I'm curious.

"He cried. I've never seen him cry. He's devastated. He kept saying, 'I can't believe she did this.'"

I still see the painful expression on his face when I told him the news. I wish I could've handled breaking up with him differently. I panicked. I discarded him like he meant nothing. He didn't deserve it. If I weren't pregnant, I think I'd still be with Gregory. Right now, we'd be celebrating my performance from last night. I don't drink, but I know I'd be with him on his boat partying with the crew the way we did this past Fourth of July.

"Why, Maddie?" she asks.

"Why what?" I respond.

"Why JB? I told you about him."

"You did, but there's a side of him you don't see."

"Why do think they call him Wolf?" she asks.

"Because he huffs and puffs." I recall the explanation he gave me for the name given to him by his fraternity brothers.

Cassandra glares at me. "He told you that?" she asks.

"He admitted he was a wolf, but he was changing."

"And you believed him?"

"He told me I was different."

"What makes you different, Maddie?"

"It's hard for me to explain, but he said I was the best thing he ever had."

"Stop." She covers her ears.

No one can fully understand the dynamics of our situation unless they are there in the moment with us.

"He's so talented, and that's what I like about him," I say.

"Gregory's talented. Name another Black guy who can single-handedly navigate a fifty-foot yacht."

"Yes. That requires skill, but piano prowess is talent of a different kind—the kind that I like."

"But Gregory's family's connected."

"So is JB's."

"Not like the Washingtons. Yeah, JB's dad played with the Lakers, and even JB has a shot at the pros, but Gregory's family has money—lots of it. If JB gets hurt, what can he do besides play basketball?"

"You have to see it to understand."

"See what?" She gives me the side-eye.

I chuckle because I know what she's thinking, and that's the furthest thing from my mind. The energy I get when I'm around JB is like the kind I feel when I enter the stage before a performance. My heart races, my adrenaline flows, butterflies take over, my palms sweat. It's as if I'm flying when my feet haven't left the ground. Seeing the way music just flows through him is something I wish everyone could experience. Watching JB so beautifully articulate thoughts and melodies is like watching a graceful figure skater land a perfect triple jump.

"Earlier, when he was here, he sang me a song he just made up. I was nauseous, I felt awful but the minute he started singing, I felt so much better."

"All he has to do is sing and *poof* all your problems gone—just like that?"

I'm glaring at her. The room is quiet except for a low hum coming from the central air conditioning. Then Cassandra asks, "Does Caleb know?"

"Yes," I answer.

"Let's say Caleb and JB are at an away game, and after the game, they get to the hotel, and Caleb sees JB fooling around. Do you think Caleb will tell you? Will he keep the peace to protect JB or end their friendship altogether?"

I let those words sink in. "I wouldn't want to be the reason they end their friendship."

I feared this happening once Caleb found out. JB and I even had this discussion. I was off limits to JB because of his reputation with the girls, plus he was in a relationship with someone. I wasn't trying to get that close to him, but it was our love for the piano that connected us.

"Remember Kyle's leaving for Fisk, and his party is tomorrow. I still want you to come but Kyle's upset with you."

"So, he doesn't want me there?" I ask.

She nods.

He and Gregory are friends, so I get it, even if I don't like it.

Cassandra moves across the bed and places a hand over my stomach. "I've never been this close to anybody pregnant before," she says.

I sigh. "You haven't? Wow. I've seen pregnant women at my father's church, but of course they have husbands."

"What does your daddy say?"

"Marry JB."

I notice Cassandra's right eyebrow raise instantly. "That's insane. What's wrong with him?"

"Daddy believes marriage makes our situation legitimate."

"No. No. No. Only a fool would be crazy enough to marry JB. Don't be a fool, Maddie."

"You make it sound like he's a really horrible person when he's not."

"I've watched him and Caleb change girls like underwear—from movie star types to cheerleader types to older women and girls around the way. He even messed around with Mona's older sister, and this was recent."

My ears ring with that news. "How recent?"

"During the basketball season."

"That doesn't tell me how recent."

"This year. Before you came."

"Oh."

"And he's with Basha, too."

"JB says they were finished."

"And you believe him?"

Cassandra is only sixteen years old, but I swear she thinks like someone twice her age. Growing up in a household where the rules weren't as strict allowed her a chance to experience some things. Unlike myself, my life was the piano and not much else, and when I finally get my chance at freedom, I overdid it. Pregnant after the first time.

"Don't judge me, Cassandra."

"Too late."

"He has no reason to lie to me."

She sighs. "You have no idea what you've gotten yourself involved in."

"Time will tell," is my reply.

Later that night as I lay tossing and turning, I feel like life has me by the neck, strangling the very essence out of me. It's like I'm dying when I really haven't had an opportunity to live. It's 11:48 p.m. I turn on the lamp and retrieve JB's number from my book of compositions. It's there scribbled on a piece of notebook paper ripped from a tablet that Aunt Mary keeps inside an end table next to the sofa. I listen for the tone and dial his number, and I wait and wait and wait.

And as I wait, I tell myself, *If he picks up, it's meant to be; if he doesn't, then everything Cassandra says about him is true.*

"Hello," he finally answers.

"Hi."

"What's up?"

"I can't sleep," I tell him.

"Me either."

"What are you doing?" I ask.

"Writing about you."

"You're just saying that."

"I have a song in my head. I wish you were here so we could go over it together."

"Can you play it, and I write down the notes?" I ask.

I hear chords intricately woven together and executed in the stylings of a jazz pianist.

"Sounds like a G chord," I say.

"I don't know what that means, but if you say so," he responds.

"Play it again."

I listen, taking notes on my end. If I were there, I would add a different note to give the melody a different voicing. I hear him singing:

"You are so incredibly talented." I'm gushing, and although I've been awake for nearly eighteen hours, listening to JB's voice gives me a second wind, reviving and breathing life back into me. "I wish I was with you," I say.

"I'll be there in less than five minutes," he says before quickly hanging up, not giving me a chance to respond.

My heart starts racing. *What just happened?* Something takes over me, and without hesitation, I open my closet to grab my duffle and pack some toiletries along with a change of clothing. My daddy and Gilda are back at the hotel. JB's parents returned home. Aunt Mary and Uncle Frenchy are asleep. Cassandra is now asleep. When I walk downstairs with my duffle bag in tow, my cousin Caleb is sitting at the bar eating. I'm on edge, and my ears start ringing. He notices me then glances at his watch.

"Damn. You must be sleepwalking," he says.

"I need to get out," I answer.

"But it's after midnight."

I don't answer.

"It's after midnight," he repeats.

"I know this."

He notices my duffle. "Where are you going?"

"JB's coming by," I tell him.

He frowns. "No way."

I nod, and for the strangest reason I feel emboldened, like I'm an adult and it's my business.

"I don't like you being with him," Caleb says.

"But I like him a lot."

"Should've hipped you to him."

"He's not a bad person."

"He's not the right person for you, though."

"I think he is."

"Did you tell Mom and Frenchy you were leaving?"

"I'm coming right back."

"Cuzzo, that's not what I asked."

"You know I didn't tell them."

Caleb is fair complected, like his sister, Cassandra, and when both are upset, they turn eight shades of red. He rises from his chair. He's six-eight, the same height as JB.

"When he comes, I'ma rough him up," he declares.

"Caleb, come on. Just talk to him, please."

"He crossed the line."

"But things happen, Caleb. JB didn't force me to do anything I didn't already want to do."

He must've sensed JB's presence or heard his car door slam because as soon as he opens the front door, JB is there. Caleb startles him.

"Oh shit," I hear JB utter before my cousin punches him in the face.

JB grabs his jaw, stumbling back onto the driveway. Caleb pounces on him swinging and punching before JB does a quick maneuver, and now, he has an upper advantage. They roll on the pavement until they are on the grass, both cursing and tussling. I'm glad it's nighttime, and even if the porchlight is on, the neighbors are asleep. I'm struggling to pull them apart, trying hard not to scream but wanting them to stop. I grab my duffle and swing, hitting Caleb in the back. Startled, he glares at me; his nostrils are flaring.

"Stop," I plead.

He and JB slowly get back on their feet. Both their chests are heaving from the pandemonium.

"You're lucky I didn't pound your freaking head in this pavement," he says to JB, spit spraying from his lips.

JB holds his jaw, moving it from side to side. I imagine it's stinging from Caleb's jab. "Damn, dude. You didn't have to bumrush me. Let's talk this shit out," he manages to say.

"It's after midnight. You're at my house, and my cousin has a duffle bag. What? You planned to sneak her out hoping you wouldn't get caught?"

"She called me," JB says. "What's the worst that could happen?" He grabs my duffle bag and drapes it over his shoulder. "She ends up pregnant?"

I follow him to his car where he opens the passenger door for me. I see Caleb standing in front of the car. The sarcasm isn't lost on him. He's speechless. The porchlight behind casts him like a tall shadow. I see the outline of his head following JB to the driver's side of the car.

"That's so disrespectful," Caleb says.

JB opens the door, sits inside, and starts the engine.

Caleb walks up signaling me to let down my window. "Is this what you want?" he asks.

I nod. "Yes."

"Damn. I'm out of it." He backs away, holding up his hands.

Caleb's always been my protector. In his eyes, I can do no wrong. I feel guilty for letting him down. Although it's dark out and I can't see his eyes, I sense the disappointment, and to me, that hurts.

# Three

JB lives in the same neighborhood, a short distance from where I'm staying. We're in his driveway within minutes.

"Are your parents asleep?" I ask.

"Finally," JB answers. "After we left your aunt's house, they got into a huge argument. Pops is angry at Mom because she didn't come to his defense."

"I like your mother. She's really sweet."

"Pops is cool too. He's been around, so he's seen how ugly paternity gets when it comes to high-profile athletes. He's just looking out."

I'm a little hesitant, second-guessing myself for coming here. I don't want to tell JB to take me back home. Part of me wants to be around him and see where the night takes us, creative-wise. He takes my hand and leads me to the side of the house. He unlocks a gate, and I see the blue light emanating from the pool. The smell of the chlorine fills my nostrils. Smitty, his Ibizan hound, runs up to me, sniffing my scent and licking my legs. I bend to rub and pet his coat. Memories of this summer flood my mind, and I'm thinking, *Here I go again.*

JB flips on the light to the pool house, and I notice the keyboard. Sitting on top is his worn black-and-white speckled composition notebook of songs and other papers with words scribbled across them. He's still moving his jaw from side to side. There are grass stains on the back of his shirt and scrapes on his elbows from rolling and fighting on the pavement.

"Your cousin tried to take my head off," he says, walking into the bathroom, which is where I follow him. He opens the medicine cabinet to retrieve a bottle of rubbing alcohol and a cotton ball.

I see his reflection in the mirror and notice a bruise on the left side of his face where Caleb punched him. He notices it, too, rubbing it before putting a cotton ball up to the bottle's opening. I watch him rub a cut and see him tense from the sting of the alcohol.

"Let me help," I say before taking the bottle of rubbing alcohol and cotton ball and applying it to the areas where I see cuts and scrapes. He takes off his shirt, and my heart does somersaults. His body is lean and ripped—like a sculptor took a carving knife and with great care and meticulous eyes carved each muscle in perfect precision. I forget about the cuts, and my hand glides over his stomach. I can feel the definition of his abs and the warmth of his skin. From the mirror's reflection, we lock eyes.

"I hope you guys mend your friendship," I say.

"It's not broken—at least not to me," he replies.

"I don't ever want to see you and Caleb fighting again."

"We're good. He needed to get it out of his system."

"Tonight Caleb asked me if being with you was what I wanted."

He's looking at my reflection in the mirror. I notice his eyes linger at my lips as I speak.

"No one could possibly see the side of you that I experienced," I tell him.

He nods, listening as I go on.

"I can't help thinking that he also meant that being with you means having to compete with basketball, other girls, and all the attention."

"My world is crazy. Once I call this agent..." He pauses. "It will get even crazier."

I can't help the sinking feeling in my stomach, which has more to do with anxiety than nausea.

He puts the top back on the rubbing alcohol and tosses the blood-and-dirt–soaked cotton ball into a wastebasket.

"I'm about to shower. Want to join me?" he asks before opening the shower door and reaching in to turn the faucet.

"I'll be in the next room playing on your keyboard," I say.

I'm taken back to this summer and all the feelings and emotions I felt being around him. He stands, waiting in case I change my mind as steam from the hot shower fills the space.

I slowly walk back into the room, leaving him standing in a thick cloud of steam. I notice the sofa pulled out into a bed with sheets folded back and pillows fluffed. I sit before the keyboard and look at what he's written. I shift my focus to the black-and-white speckled, composition notebook—the one where he says all the words are about me. I open it and thumb through pages. I read the following: *I love her, like no other, she's the one for me. We make love, we make music, always in the perfect key.* I see drawings of a black silhouette in the shape of my body, and I read: *When she calls my name. It drives me wild. There's nothing better than the sweet sound of making love. She's lying in my arms. I keep her safe and warm. I love how she feels. This girl of mine is real.* I flip through more pages and read: *Maddie, my dear, if you could only hear the pounding of my heart. It's not so hard to believe, how much joy to me you bring. Your vibe is innocent. Your energy is real. Words do no justice in describing how you make me feel.* I flip through more pages and read: *I choose you. When it's all said and done, I know for sure you are the real one.* I hear a melody to these lyrics. Notes churning, chords coming together. I read more: *Late summer when you told me. Never imagined it would be this soon. Our lives are about to change. Maybe we should jump the broom.*

*Jump the broom?*

My heart races. JB is writing about marriage. *Who's thinking about marriage at seventeen and twenty? We are.*

These butterflies I feel I can't stop. My heart has a mind of its own. I'm remembering the melody JB played earlier, and I get a blank staff sheet. I'm reading the words *jump the broom,* and I hear melodies combined with the water from the shower. My creative juices are activated, and I start writing, then I play a little just to hear how it all comes together. I close my eyes, and the notes and melodies cover me like a handmade quilt. I stop to write them down before I resume playing. I'm hearing the notes from another song I composed, and I combine them. I'm playing the song when JB enters with a bath towel wrapped around his waist. He approaches and listens while I play.

"I think I have something," I say to him.

"Cool. I have something, too." He sits next to me at the keyboard, and I smell the clean, airy scent of soap. He leans in close and kisses my neck. "I missed you," he whispers. "It's been a long time for us."

I stop playing and embrace him, squeezing him to the point I feel bone and muscle. We kiss, and it's frantic, like it's the end of the world. I don't know why, but I start crying. I hear myself sob. So many emotions I can't pinpoint just one. He picks me up and carries me to the sofa bed. I don't think about the hours and days ahead. All I think about is now.

*** 

My eyes adjust, and I see sunlight peeking through the shutters, then I hear the toilet flush, and seconds later, water flowing from the faucet.

JB missed me. He missed every part and every inch of me. When he climbs back into bed, he still misses me. Music plays on the stereo, a song with a sweet, simple melody by a rapper he calls LL Cool J.

"I like that song," I whisper, running my fingers through his hair while he kisses me.

"I Need Love," he whispers back.

"You do?" I answer.

"That's the name of the song," he says.

"It's nice. What happened to the song we're supposed to work on?" I ask.

"You tell me," he says, appearing to savor every kiss, looking at me, anticipating an answer.

"I really wanted to work on it. What was the song about?"

"Us." He stops kissing me. I examine the bruise on his face.

"What about us?" I ask.

"When I found out you were pregnant," he answers.

"Horrifying."

"I was hoping and praying you were on the pill."

"Oh God, how I wish."

There's a brief silence, except for the music playing softly from the stereo's speakers.

"You felt so good though," he says between more kisses. "My mind was saying, 'C'mon get out,' but the other part was saying, 'Let's do this. It's right, it's tight, and damnit this could go all night.'"

"You're so silly."

As sweet and tender as the moment is, I shudder when I think of the reaction from Aunt Mary and Uncle Frenchy when they find out I spent the night.

"What time is it?" I ask.

"It's a quarter after nine," he responds.

"I've got to go."

"Yeah, me too. I didn't realize today was the last day to register for the fall semester," JB answers.

"You're going back to school?" I ask.

"Yes."

"When are you going to call your agent?"

"Everything has to be done at the right time."

"I see."

"There's so much happening. About a month ago, I had an opportunity to try out for a spot on the U.S. Olympic team. Now, I'm waiting to hear back from them."

"Olympics? How does that work?"

"I make the team, represent my country, play for an Olympic gold medal, and get on a box of Wheaties."

"When will you play?"

"September '88 in Seoul, South Korea."

"South Korea?"

He notices the anxiety and fear in my expression.

"I have to make the team. Stop worrying, okay?" he says before kissing me once again. The music stops.

\*\*\*

JB and I find Aunt Mary and Uncle Frenchy poolside, reading newspapers. They both look up from their papers then at each other.

"Just the people we want to see. Pull up a chair," Uncle Frenchy says.

"I can't stay but a minute," JB tells them.

"Oh, this won't take long," Uncle Frenchy insists.

JB pulls up chairs for the both of us. I never told Uncle Frenchy about the pregnancy, but I get the feeling he knows.

"You two got some damn nerve," he says.

I take a deep breath and exhale. Why does this feel worse than the moment Daddy found out? I'm tearing up again, and although I think I'm at a point where I can manage the nausea, I feel it coming.

JB begins, "First, let me start off by saying, I'm sorry. I *uhhh...*" He searches for words, "got caught up."

Uncle Frenchy notices the bruise on JB's face. "What happened?"

"It's nothing," he answers.

"Doesn't look like nothing to me," Aunt Mary replies.

"Caleb and I got into a scuffle. We're good now."

"I'm surprised you're not in a hospital getting an operation to remove your daddy's size fifteen shoe from your butt," Uncle Frenchy says.

"He's not happy," JB mumbles.

"None of us are. What were y'all thinking?" Uncle Frenchy leans forward.

JB is silent. Embarrassed, my guess.

Uncle Frenchy looks at me to respond. I clear my throat. "I'm sorry" is all I have to say.

"Mary and I promised your daddy to look after you. Now we look like liars, and I don't like it."

"I understand," I whisper.

"Cassandra checks your bed, and it's empty. We find out from Caleb you're gone with JB." He looks at us, gauging our reaction.

"It won't happen again," JB assures them.

"You're absolutely right about that." As he's scolding us, I see where Caleb and Cassandra get their angry shade of red from. "Maddie, keep this up, and you'll find yourself on the flight back to Houston with your daddy."

"Yes, sir," I respond.

"This latest episode with you and JB makes us look irresponsible." Aunt Mary sighs.

I nod. "I understand."

"If you don't abide by our rules, you can't stay here," Uncle Frenchy states.

"Sorry, but I really need to run. I've got fall registration deadline," JB says to us before standing.

"You and I aren't done," Uncle Frenchy says to JB who pauses, looking perplexed, not sure what to do.

"We'll talk another time," Uncle Frenchy says to him.

JB nods. He would've given me a goodbye kiss if Aunt Mary and Uncle Frenchy weren't there. He leaves us sitting by the pool. A breeze rustles a few pages of their newspapers. Aunt Mary sips orange juice from a champagne flute and places it over the papers.

"Niecy, niecy, niecy," Uncle Frenchy begins, "you ever had a glass slip out of your hands?"

I sniff. "I have."

"Even when you think you've cleaned up the mess, you still find shards in random spots, and if you're not careful and you happen to be barefoot, you step on one. Painful, isn't it?"

I nod. "Yes."

"This affects us all," he says.

"I was just thinking, maybe I should start looking for another place to stay," I hear myself utter.

"You have any idea how much it costs to rent out here? It's not Texas," Aunt Mary answers.

"We're not putting you out, but know while you're here, you have rules. You're familiar with them," Uncle Frenchy reiterates.

The rules: Be home by 11:30, no drugs, no sex, no strange characters. I don't want to be where I'm hampered by rules that I've pretty much broken. I want my own space, big enough for a piano. I would love the baby grand Aunt Mary had at the youth center. I want my space to be within walking distance of the beach, where I can sit in the sand for hours, and I can be inspired by the cries of the seagulls or the rush of the waves. When evening comes, I want to watch the sun set alone or with JB.

Daddy and Gilda arrive around one. We sit in the entertainment room where I used to spend hours practicing my Schumann piece on the family's black baby grand piano. Where we now sit, I get a crazy flashback of the time Gregory arrived from Europe, and we kissed and cuddled. I get a butterfly sensation remembering the moment we paused for air just to gaze into each other's eyes.

"The phone in my hotel room's been ringing nonstop. Everyone is still talking about your stellar performance and the terrible fall you suffered on stage. I talked to the conductor and members of the philharmonic. They asked about you, and I told them you were well and resting. You received rave reviews. They want to schedule a meeting with you." Gilda places her glasses on the tip of her nose.

"L.A. Phil wants to have a meeting with me?" I ask.

"Absolutely," Gilda says. "The meeting could result in the possibility of a guest pianist position. Isn't that great?"

"That is awesome, Gilda. Thank you."

"I have to figure out how to work this around the pregnancy."

"What's my schedule between now and December?"

She opens a briefcase and retrieves papers. "These are contracts for four performances in Washington, D.C., and Philadelphia for the second and third weekends of December."

I read over the contracts while she continues. "I called Juilliard to inform them that you've decided to put your studies on hold."

"Did you tell them why?"

"Personal family matters," she answers.

"Will they hold my spot?"

"No. You have to repeat the in-person audition and take the music theory exam again."

I'm thinking, *What if I'm still pregnant during the audition? Will they judge me? What if I don't make it this time?* I'm reading the contract. I see the dollar amount that the D.C. company is paying for two performances, and I'm already thinking of what I can do with the money.

"I want to move out and get my own place," I blurt.

Gilda and Daddy remain quiet.

"Did your aunt and uncle encourage you to move?" Daddy asks.

"No, I...*ummm*...just think with everything's that's happened, it's best I had my own place. Besides, I need space where I can play my music when I get inspired. I can't do that at Aunt Mary's and Uncle Frenchy's."

Daddy rests his chin in his hand, and he looks exhausted.

"I want to tell you before you hear it from someone else that I spent the night with JB," I confess.

Daddy sighs. "You did what?"

"Last night after you all left, I spent the night with JB."

Daddy takes a minute to let my words sink in. "How does it look, me ministering to thousands about the virtues of Christian living. Meanwhile my daughter is seventeen, pregnant, not married, and fornicating every chance she gets."

"Would it make you feel better if I said you're not the only minister with these problems?"

"Do you understand decency and order?" he asks.

"Yes, Daddy."

"What does it mean to you, Maddie?"

I'm silent.

"Maybe you need to come back home to Houston," he says.

"No. Then people will ask why I'm not at Juilliard, and soon they'll see why. I don't want to go back; it'll just remind me that I've failed."

"You haven't failed. That's not what you did. You took a detour." Daddy says.

"Can we look for a place?" I'm pleading.

"You're not old enough to sign a lease" is his response.

"But you or Gilda can sign it for me."

"Leave Gilda out of this," Daddy goes on to say. "Continue to stay with your uncle and aunt, or pack up your things and come back to Houston with us."

A lump enters my throat. Just the idea of going back to Houston depresses me. I've got to find me another plan. Quick.

The rest of the day and into the evening, we talk with Aunt Mary about my upcoming doctor's appointment. We found a doctor, and my first appointment is a week from today. As Daddy and Gilda prepare to leave and go back to the hotel, Cassandra is dressed and ready to go to Kyle's party. Her hair is straightened, and she's wearing a blue metallic off-the-shoulder top with a white skirt and blue pumps.

"This feels weird," she says to me.

I walk with her outside to her car, and I notice the crack in the windshield. About a month ago, we were leaving a skating rink in Compton when we got caught in the pathway of a high-speed chase.

"Uncle Frenchy and Aunt Mary know about this?" I ask, pointing to the windshield.

"I lied and told them an eighteen-wheeler hit a pile of rocks on the expressway." She shrugs before getting into the car.

"Take pictures." I close the door.

"With what? I don't have a camera," she replies.

"Why didn't you bring it?"

"I don't want to carry that thing around with me."

I notice her eyes blurring with tears.

"Are you okay?" I ask.

"Everything is different now that you're—" She starts up the engine and wipes away a tear.

I take a deep breath and step away from the car watching her drive off until I can no longer see it. The neighborhood is quiet as the evening sun sets, and in the distance, I hear the roar of the traffic and the sound of a chopper overhead. The neighborhood sits in the hills with the most amazing views of Los Angeles. I can look out my window and see the sun set. I love sunsets, especially when the sky turns orange, purple, and red. What's more beautiful is watching the sun set while on the beach. I've watched it, wrapped in JB's arms; I've watched it sitting on Gregory's yacht. Right now, I'm inspired to write about it and play it on the family's piano. I grab my staff sheets and listen for the notes, writing them, imagining each one dipped in a color. If red had a sound, how do I describe it? Is it loud? Jarring? Does it crackle like flames licking firewood? Would red ooze like blood from the bell of a clarinet? That's what I hear a clarinet, slowly descending like the sun until all that's left are the different hues. When darkness settles, the piano plays, and I improvise, seeing the color black. I tickle the high notes. They remind me of stars, bright and white. When I'm composing a song, I get so lost in the music that I forget about the time. I hear raised voices coming from the other room. I look at the clock, and it's a little after midnight. I stop playing and listen.

# Four

I open the door to see Cassandra and Aunt Mary at the base of the stairs. Aunt Mary's in her robe.

"You're not going to the after-party. Haven't you partied enough?" Aunt Mary says to her.

"Mom, it's Kyle's last night in town. Please."

"I know. I also know it's past your curfew."

"Please. I promise after tonight I won't ask you for anything else."

Without saying a word, Aunt Mary points upstairs.

Cassandra pouts and bounds for the stairs. Her heels click hard and deliberate against the hardwood floor. Seconds later, I hear the door slam to her room. Aunt Mary turns to me and the look of consternation for Cassandra turns to disappointment with a slow sigh for me.

"I hear you hammering away. You should be exhausted," she says.

"I wasn't aware of the time."

The phone rings, and suddenly my heart pounds.

"Who's calling at this ungodly hour?" She makes a dash for the phone before it can ring a second time.

"Hello?" I notice her eyes searching the room as she listens to the voice. From her receiver, I can clearly hear JB apologizing.

"Some of us are sleeping," she says. "Yes. She happens to be awake." She holds out the handset for me.

"Thank you," I say before taking it and finding a spot on the sofa. I watch her turn off lights before she climbs the stairs, leaving me alone in semi-darkness.

"Hello."

"After I left, did your uncle and aunt start trippin'?" he asks.

"Of course."

"I figured as much."

"I got lectured on the house rules, which has me thinking I want my own place."

"Word?"

"Somewhere near the beach."

"I got a frat whose dad has a townhouse rental. He's looking for a tenant. It's in Santa Monica so rent's a lot, but something tells me you can handle it."

"Will you arrange something? I'd love to see it."

"I'll make it happen." The way he says that leaves me without a doubt.

"My first appointment with the obstetrician is next Thursday at 10:45."

"Next Thursday?" he repeats. "I have class."

"No. You can't miss this."

"My schedule is crazy."

"Crazy how?" I ask.

"I've got a full course load, practice usually lasts two hours, my workouts last a couple of hours, I'm in meetings with the coach, I'm studying film and plays, I'm talking to reporters, I'm busy with my fraternity, I'm doing community work. I'm checking on Dee."

"Dee." My heart sinks when he mentions her name. Right now, Dee is a nine-year-old girl at UCLA hospital fighting for her life. In June, Dee was diagnosed with bone cancer. It's been aggressive. She was a regular at Aunt Mary's youth center who I had grown close with. In so many ways, she reminded me of myself at nine. I started to teach her the piano, and she was so eager to learn—until her diagnosis.

"Let's see her this weekend," JB says, and from the relaxed tone of his voice, I can tell he's lying down. I imagine him stretched across his waterbed, wearing only athletic shorts, his eyes are closed, and his hands rubbing his abs.

"I wrote a composition about sunsets," I tell him.

"Word? I want to hear it."

"You will—soon."

We end our conversation on that note. While lying on the sofa, my thoughts drift to this morning, waking up next to him. How I fantasize of doing that every day, feeling his soft curls around my fingers, gazing into his eyes and hearing him sing me a song he improvised.

I knock on Cassandra's door and find she's still awake and brushing her hair.

"I'll do it," I say, holding out my hand for her to give me the brush. Most of the time, it's her brushing my hair.

"Tell me all about the party," I say before gathering and brushing a handful of her strands. Her hair is sandy-brown and fine, so the strands slip easily through my fingers.

"A lot of our friends from Harvard and Westlake were there. Only you and Mona were missing."

"What about Gregory?"

"He shows up with a date, so Ursula's asks, 'What's up? Where's Maddie?' He says, 'We're done.' Ursula's crushed."

"He told her why we broke up?"

"I don't know."

"His date, how did she look?"

"White, blonde, big fake boobs. She wore a cute Versace corset dress. She was all over Gregory."

"And what about him?"

"He seemed preoccupied, like he really wasn't into her—almost like she was someone to pass the time with."

"Does she attend Westlake?" I ask, just a little curious.

"I think she's graduated."

"You and Kyle say your goodbyes?"

"Not officially. After Kyle's party ended, I came home to ask Mom for permission to meet Kyle and Gregory and some other people in Brentwood."

"What's happening there?" I ask.

"Another party. This one without the adult supervision. But because of that stupid curfew of hers, I can't go. So no, I never got to officially say goodbye to him."

"When is he leaving?"

"Tomorrow."

"Then you still have time."

"No, I won't," Cassandra says.

I stop brushing her hair.

"Why did you stop?"

"Our crew." The thought of everyone leaving hits me, and my eyes blur with tears.

Cassandra turns around. "Are you crying?"

"I don't know why this is so emotional," I say, wiping away a tear.

Cassandra dabs away a tear. "It's your hormones."

"Maybe it is."

"I'd be freaking out if I were you."

"I'm staying positive."

"I was freaking out this morning when I didn't see you, then I found out where you were." She gives me an eye roll.

"Don't judge me," I respond.

"I'm not saying anything." She grabs her eye mask and places it over her face.

The following afternoon, I ride with Cassandra to the airport to say goodbye to Kyle. Kyle's parents are there. When I approach Kyle and his family to say hello, Kyle is dry. I admit, it stings a little. I told Cassandra I needed to stay home, but she insisted I come. She wanted her hand held the way she held mine the day I cried my eyes out after Gregory left for Europe.

Cassandra takes this opportunity to say her final goodbyes to Kyle. It's emotional. I'm getting misty eyed watching them hug. The airline agent announces the flight number bound for Nashville. Kyle hugs his parents. Kyle's hug and goodbye for me are still dry, and my feelings are quite hurt. Meanwhile Cassandra's standing at the window, tears flowing. Kyle's mother gives her a tissue, and together they cry.

Minutes later, we're sitting in the car. She grips the steering wheel. "Maddie, what am I going to do?" she cries. "I never got to *officially* say goodbye to him."

"Yes, you did."

"No, I didn't."

"I'm confused."

"I wanted to give him a goodbye present," she says before she starts the car, and off we drive.

"Oh, now I see what you're saying. You wanted to have sex."

"Why not?" she says.

"I'm not saying you shouldn't have, but...you'll have other times," I say.

We zip through traffic, driving through an exclusive neighborhood before we eventually pull into the driveway of a vine-encrusted English country manor house. It sits on a slight knoll with an imposing street presence. A female house employee answers the door and leads us outside to the pool where Ursula lies topless.

"Miss Woods, you have guests," she announces.

Ursula reaches for a towel to wrap herself. Cassandra and I sit in a pair of lounge chairs.

"What happened with you and Gregory?" She skips formalities and jumps right in.

I sigh. "We broke up."

"Why?"

I take a deep breath. I guess Gregory didn't tell her.

"Promise you won't mention this to anyone else."

I pause. She's listening intently to what I'm about to say.

"I'm pregnant."

Ursula's mouth drops. "No way."

I nod.

"No way, Maddie."

Again, I nod.

"You are kidding me."

I'm silent. Her reaction is like others' reactions when they hear the news.

"Is it Gregory's?" she asks, stammering.

I shake my head. Her eyes widen.

"It's a long story," I tell her and leave it at that.

"Are you going to keep me guessing?"

"I'm not saying."

She studies me for a minute before she reaches out to place a hand on my stomach. "I'm here for you."

She gives me a hug. Ursula's words make me emotional and teary-eyed.

"You're not going through this alone," she says.

Cassandra sits next to me. She's pensive. "And although I'm upset for reasons you already know, I'm here for you too."

"Thank you. It means a lot," I tell her.

Cassandra sobs, which I believe has more to do with Kyle leaving than my situation.

"Stop," Ursula says while fanning back tears.

"Kyle left today." Cassandra's face is the color of a fire truck.

"Can I share something with you?" Ursula begins. "Long-distance relationships don't work."

"That's not true." Cassandra continues to wipe tears.

"Once he gets to Fisk, he'll forget about you."

"You're making me feel horrible," Cassandra says.

"It's a fact," Ursula says.

"What am I going to do?"

"When you graduate, go to Nashville," Ursula suggests.

"Hell no."

Ursula and I are amused at how quickly she changes her tune when we mention Nashville.

"If you really cared about him, you would." Ursula tucks in her towel.

"Maybe if he went to Howard," Cassandra replies.

Ursula turns her attention to me. "I'm still shocked. Are you keeping it?"

"I am."

"Why?"

I think of all the baby dedication and christening ceremonies that have taken place at the church and the one thing Daddy always reiterated.

"A baby is a blessing," I answer.

"Yes, when it's planned." Ursula takes a long pause. "Would you consider adoption?"

"No." Tears fill my eyes as I imagine a nurse taking a crying newborn baby out of my arms.

"How far along are you?" Ursula asks.

"Eight weeks."

"What about Juilliard? You know, Mona's in New York City."

Ursula mentions our other friend Mona who's a fashion model and actress.

"They're not holding my spot, so I'll have to repeat the process again," I tell her.

"Good luck with that." Ursula runs a hand through her wet, curly hair. "I'm taking a year off to travel."

"Where?" I ask.

"Spain, Italy, Greece, and maybe the South of France."

"Alone?" Cassandra asks.

"Of course," Ursula responds.

"How's Oliver?" Cassandra asks.

"We're good."

Oliver used to be one of our camp counselors a couple of years back. He and Ursula started dating this past summer.

"And Harry the comedian?" Cassandra asks again.

Harry was another guy Ursula was seeing.

I notice an eye roll. "He's fine. These days, he's busy working on another movie."

"Is he acting? Directing? Writing?" Cassandra asks.

"All of it," she answers. "He tells me it's a spoof of 1970s blaxploitation films."

"Interesting," Cassandra responds.

"It's Friday. Any plans this weekend?" Ursula asks, anxious to change the subject. "I saw a trailer for this new movie called *Dirty Dancing*. You guys want to see it?" she asks.

"It'll remind me of Kyle." Cassandra sticks out her lip.

"Never mind," Ursula says.

I run a hand through my hair. My brown-chestnut color with highlights have faded, and I'm wondering if it's even safe to color it now that I'm pregnant.

"Tomorrow, let's do a pamper day with lunch," I suggest.

"Yes, manis and pedis." Ursula waves her hands like a fan.

"I chipped a couple of nails when I fell." I glance at my right index and middle fingers.

"Ursula, I like your place on Melrose. They soak your feet in rose water," Cassandra gushes.

"They've also installed state-of-the-art recliners that massage your back while you get your mani-pedis. I've fallen asleep a few times," Ursula adds.

"What's happening tonight? What's Harry doing at the Comedy Club?" Cassandra asks.

"I told you he's working on a movie," Ursula replies.

"I don't want to go home. I'll think about Kyle and get depressed."

"Then stay here. Don't worry about clothes—we're identical sizes. Besides, I have clothes with the tags still on."

"What about me?" I ask, remembering this summer at our friend Mona's family's beach property in Malibu. They were trying on clothing, and everyone was in size three juniors, tall, and slender with bodies like models. Me, I'm five-foot-three with 40DD breasts, a twenty-seven-inch waist with forty-one-inch hips. I've gained a little weight, so now I am a size twelve in misses.

JB thinks it's sexy, and he says I've got the body of a real woman. But being in L.A. where it seems most girls are model-thin, I'm more self-conscious. Now that I'm pregnant, I can't imagine how much more I'll gain. Just thinking about it is depressing.

"Oh Maddie, I'm sorry." Ursula's expression is genuinely crushed.

"It's okay." Inside, I'm miserable. *Maddie, you are so beautiful, but you need to push away from the table. Maddie, you have a gorgeous face. Too bad you can't fit into that size five Max V dress.*

"Once I start working out and eating right, I'll be a size three, watch."

"Of course" is Ursula's response. She's really thinking, *Yeah, right.*

There is brief silence, except for the birds chirping in the elm trees.

"Tell us about the after party in Brentwood," Cassandra says.

"Kyle was sad you couldn't make it."

"Because of Mom and her stupid curfew," Cassandra says.

"Did you have a curfew, Maddie?"

"I did."

"Your pregnancy is mind blowing," Ursula says. "Who is the father again?"

"I'm not saying."

"Anyone I know?"

"I'm not saying."

"Really?"

I glance at Cassandra who looks away. "What?" I ask.

"I'm not saying anything," Cassandra says.

"Oh my, the suspense is killing me," Ursula announces.

The rest of the evening, she looks at me, hoping I slip and mention his name. My lips remain sealed—for now.

# Five

I thought I was dreaming about ringing a bell, but it was the telephone. Moments later, Aunt Mary enters the room. She flicks on the bedroom light.

"How soon can you get dressed?" she asks.

My eyes are struggling to adjust as I'm disoriented when I read the clock and see 5:23.

"What's happening?"

"That was Dee's mom, Felicia. Dee's condition has worsened."

Upon hearing that, my heart races. A dropping sensation overtakes my body. I manage to get out of bed, and without missing a beat, I wash my face, brush my teeth, and take a quick shower. As soon as I get out of the shower, here comes the nausea. I fall to my knees, hugging the toilet. Tears flood my eyes. I say a prayer. I continue my prayers in the car on the way to the hospital. When we arrive, Felicia is by Dee's bedside holding Dee's hand to her lips, kissing and pressing it against her cheek. Dee's breathing is shallow, and the beep from the heart monitor is slow.

Felicia and I embrace. I feel her hands rubbing my back. Seeing Dee now and remembering how she was just months ago leaves me with an aching feeling.

"She really likes you, Maddie. You made her look forward to coming to the youth center."

We pull apart. "She is such a beautiful little girl. You gave her the perfect name: Delight."

Felicia forces herself to smile. "Where's JB? You might want to call and tell him to get here," she says.

I glance at Aunt Mary, feeling as if I still need her approval. She nods. I walk outside the room to the nearest phone to dial his number. I hope I catch him before he goes out for his run. He picks up on the fourth ring.

"JB, it's Maddie. I'm at UCLA. How soon can you get here?"

"Is Dee okay?" he asks after a pause.

Holding the handset, my voice catches. "I don't know."

"I'm on the way" is all he says before hanging up.

I hurry down the corridor back the room to find Felicia now sitting next to Dee's bed. Aunt Mary sits nearby. I pull up a chair next to Aunt Mary. She takes my hand. We sit quietly.

"Maddie," I hear Felicia say, "can you play something pretty?"

I blink back tears. "Of course." Under a pile of stuffed animals, I retrieve the Casio keyboard I purchased as a gift for Dee. I plug it in, turn the volume low, and play Bach's "Suite No. 1 in G Major." This piece is spiritual in tone. It flows in a way that gives hope. Closing my eyes, I feel the notes dance, and in a miraculous way, I pray Dee hears them, and they bring her back. I wish to see her healthy again. I played often for my mother when she was going through her battle with ovarian cancer. The music was soothing like pain medication.

I proceed to play another piece, Chopin's "Prelude in E Minor," one of my favorites. Often when I play, I segue into a series of other songs, and before I know, time has passed. When I play the last note and open my eyes, JB is here. He greets Felicia and Aunt Mary before giving me a hug. The scent of fresh laundry mixed with his natural mahogany teakwood aroma reminds me of a new car smell, like fine leather, very masculine. JB kneels so that he's level with Dee's bed. In a way, Dee is the reason JB and I have become close. It was mid-June when Dee suddenly became ill. I wanted to visit her, and the only available ride was JB. He accompanied me and met Dee. She liked him instantly. He won over Felicia, too.

"If she were awake, she'd be so happy to see you," Felicia says to JB.

He nods, and we all hear Dee gurgling. JB moves aside so Felicia can rejoin her bedside. A nurse enters with a physician. The nurse takes her vitals. She and the physician talk among themselves. We wait quietly to hear what they report.

"Her blood pressure has dropped, and her organs are failing," the physician says. "Miss Morris, at this juncture, we say our goodbyes. It's only a matter of time."

When Felicia closes her eyes, fresh tears roll down her cheeks. She takes Dee's hand.

"You were a good little girl. Momma tried to be the best I could. I don't want you to suffer anymore. It's okay. Momma will miss you. I love you. I love you. Momma loves you so much." She lays her head on the bedrail the very instant Dee stops breathing.

The heart monitor stops chirping, and the line goes flat. Watching this all unfold, JB wraps his arms around me, and I tell myself, *Don't break down. Stay strong for Felicia.*

Aunt Mary rubs Felicia's back, consoling her while Felicia spends the moment holding on to Dee's lifeless body.

The doctor and nurse stand by quietly. I notice the nurse wipes away a tear.

"I wanted my baby to come home," Felicia cries.

JB holds me against his chest and squeezes me tightly. Twice, I've witnessed a life slip away right before my eyes. First, my mother. Now, Dee. The feeling of helplessness overwhelms me, and my nausea makes its ugly return. I excuse myself and run to the nearest restroom.

I hold my stomach and think of the life inside me. Why is life filled with death and uncertainty? When I started volunteering at Aunt Mary's youth center this summer, I had no idea that a nine-year-old girl who reminded me of myself would teach me about life.

I wash my face and look at myself in the mirror, I remove the fastener that holds my hair together and allow all eighteen inches of it to fall past my shoulders. The reflection staring back manages a weak smile. It's still a reminder that I have light inside me. I gather myself together before I rejoin Felicia, Aunt Mary, and JB. Dee is declared dead at 9:26 a.m. The cause of death, osteosarcoma. According to doctors, it was advanced upon diagnosis. Had Dee received proper medical care prior to the diagnosis, she'd still be here.

It's surreal, watching the staff remove various drawings, JB's autographed poster, and Dee's stuffed animals. They pack them neatly in boxes and give them to us. The Casio keyboard is placed in a box, and it hits me, *She'll never be able to play it again.*

JB and a couple of the hospital staffers help load boxes of Dee's mementos into the trunk of Aunt Mary's Chevy Caprice. JB opens the passenger's door for Felicia who sits in the front seat clutching a stuffed animal.

Aunt Mary approaches us. "I'm taking Felicia home, then I'm going to see if I can get in touch with more of her family members."

"You'll need muscle," JB says.

"You forgot I ran a youth center in a war zone," she responds.

"I know, but still, you're like a second mom. I feel it's my duty," he says.

"Thanks for your concern." She glances at me. "Are you riding with us?"

"If it's okay with you, I'd like to ride with JB."

"Your father and Gilda are coming over to the house today. Let him know I'll be there at some point," Aunt Mary says before getting inside her car.

I say my goodbyes to her and Felicia before walking with JB to his car. Once inside, he grabs a towel and places it over his head.

"JB."

He holds up a finger for me to give him a moment. I sit and wait before I remove the towel. I notice his eyes are red.

"I wanted her to come home, too." He sniffs back tears.

Reality hits home for the both of us. I'm a mess—a crying, sobbing mess. He pulls me close. We embrace, and we cry.

\*\*\*

I totally forget about the mani-pedi with Ursula and Cassandra. When I tell Cassandra the news of Dee's passing, she sits and stares quietly into space.

"That is so sad," she cries. "Will you be okay?"

"I don't know," I answer.

"This is too much, I swear." Cassandra wipes away a tear.

"I had so much I wanted to share with her."

"When was the last time you saw Rosie?" Cassandra asks.

Rosie is another student who attended Aunt Mary's youth center who I became close with. She's fourteen and a gifted artist. I have her drawings kept away alongside my compositions. She drew a lot and shared her artwork with Dee. It seemed so sad to see the hospital staff remove her drawings.

"Two weeks ago, I think."

"When I spoke to her, she was talking about leaving the center, long before the incident," I say.

The incident involved a gang-related shooting. We just happened to be outside at the wrong time when it happened. A couple of the children were injured. A bullet shattered a boy's leg. It had to be amputated. He was just ten years old. Because of the shooting, Aunt Mary closed the doors of her youth center.

Rosie made me promise not to tell anyone she was living with her boyfriend and his family. When we last spoke, it sounded like her mother wasn't mentally stable, and that was her reason for moving in with him.

"She'll call—hopefully," I say, but I know if I go searching, I will find her at the Skateland roller rink in Compton.

Problem with that is Aunt Mary doesn't want us in Compton, which didn't stop us before, but we were lucky that time we made it out of Compton with only a cracked windshield.

"Are we still doing our mani-pedis with Ursula?" Cassandra asks.

"I want to, but Daddy and Gilda are coming."

"He's still in town?"

"Yes. He's flying back soon."

"I still can't believe your daddy suggested marriage to JB."

"What would you do?" I ask Cassandra.

"First, it wouldn't happen to me. Number one, I always make sure I have condoms, and number two, I'm current with my pills," she answers.

"But I wasn't having sex prior to JB."

"Come on, Maddie. You're smarter than that."

"Just never thought it would happen to me."

We end our conversation when the doorbell rings. I open the front door to see Daddy and Gilda there.

"Hello, honey," Daddy says, giving me a kiss on the cheek. "We can't stay long. Our flight is leaving in a couple of hours—plus the meter's running." I look over his shoulder and see a cab waiting at the curb. They come inside and stand in the foyer.

"Are Mary and Frenchy home?" Gilda asks.

"No. Uncle Frenchy's golfing, and Aunt Mary is with a parent. Remember the little girl we visited at UCLA?"

"I recall," he answers.

"She died this morning." I feel tears.

He sighs. "I understand you were close to her."

The reality of Dee's death hits me again. Daddy and Gilda notice, and they both bring me in close for a group hug.

"It's been a rough week," Daddy says, wiping my eyes.

Gilda reaches inside her purse to retrieve a handkerchief for me.

"I'll be okay," I assure them.

"Of course you will," Gilda says.

"I know my life is messy, but I promise I'll make you two proud of me again."

"There's a message that comes from mess," Daddy begins. "Ask yourself, 'What is my message?' It may take until next year—maybe five years—whenever to figure it out."

I walk with them outside to the waiting cab at the curb.

"I'll be back to accompany you to the first doctor's visit. I love you," he says right before he kisses my forehead.

Gilda gives me a warm, tight hug. "I'll call you once I get home," she says before sitting inside the cab and adjusting comfortably in her seat.

Daddy gets in and closes the door. I see his window going down.

"Turn your mess into a message. Do what you do best: Write a song about it," he says before the cab takes off down the hill.

*** 

It's late afternoon when Cassandra and I meet Ursula to get our mani-pedis. The Nail Salon is exclusive with privacy rooms designed for high-profile clientele. One nail tech works on my hands. The sensation from pushing and trimming my cuticles always puts me in a relaxed mood. Another nail tech works on my feet, pumicing away layers of dry skin and moisturizing them with lavender-scented oil.

"Maddie, guess who I ran into?" Ursula begins.

It can only be one person.

"Was it Gregory?"

"Yes. I was having breakfast in a French bakery not far from here when my little eye spied Gregory."

"Okay."

"I invited him to my table to talk—about you."

"You couldn't find anything else to talk about?"

"We could have, but we didn't. He's bitter."

"He'll get over it. I heard he already has," I say.

Ursula rolls her eyes and waves off the notion. "You're the girl, Maddie. He really liked you."

"I'm not getting back with Gregory."

"Why not?" Cassandra interjects. "He's better than what you have now."

I roll my eyes at Cassandra. "That's your opinion, and it doesn't matter."

"The facts I give you don't either, apparently."

"I hate how it ended—but in a way, I'm glad because I don't think I could be happy with Gregory as I am with—"

"Who?" Ursula's about to leap from her chair. "Tell me who he is."

"She's embarrassed. It took a while for her to tell me, too," Cassandra adds.

"Embarrassed? Why? Is he a midget? Is one leg shorter than the other? Does he look like The Hunchback of Notre Dame?" Ursula's badgering has all the nail techs giggling.

"No, I'm not embarrassed. I'm just not saying," I tell her.

"Ursula when you find out, you're not going to believe it" is Cassandra's reply.

This time I keep my mouth shut and watch the tech apply a base coat to my nails. Ursula takes care of the bill plus the tip when we're done.

"Thank you. Next time, my treat," I say to her before I sit in the passenger's seat of her convertible BMW. We cruise down Fairfax. It's Saturday evening in L.A. Roads are still congested, tourists still mill about, boutiques and shops are still bustling. The beaches are still crowded. We're now on Pacific Coast Highway, and we drive past the Santa Monica Pier; the Ferris wheel moves in a sloth-like motion. And like that, I think of Dee, and I am sad again. My thoughts drift in and out of the moment. One second, I'm hearing the conversation happening between Cassandra and Ursula; in a split second, I'm taken back to the hospital and the image of Felicia holding on to Dee's lifeless body.

"Remember the bonfires at Dockweiler?" Ursula asks Cassandra.

"Yes. That was our spot," Cassandra replies.

"Another spot—and I hesitate to admit—the late-night street races on Crenshaw," Ursula gushes.

"No way. You, on the Shaw? I don't believe it, Miss Hancock Park," Cassandra says.

"Met a lot of cute guys with decked-out low riders. Even took a ride in the backseat of a few," Ursula announces.

"You're wild," Cassandra declares.

They notice I haven't spoken in some time. "Maddie, why are you so quiet?" Ursula asks.

"I'm just listening" is my response, but now I'm daydreaming about JB and the minutes we spent in his car. Sitting in the hospital parking lot, we held each other close and cried. Even as I think about it, my heart flutters remembering his lips pressed against mine. We kissed. I tasted salty tears. A song with the lyrics, *"Don't disturb this groove"* played on the radio once he started the car. Between shifting gears in his old Porsche 911, he held my hand, and at times he kissed it and brushed it gently against his lips. We didn't say a lot during the ride, but I believe the little time we spent with Dee and watching her pass away right before our eyes created an unbreakable bond.

Aunt Mary and her assistant Leah arrive home shortly after Cassandra and me. If Leah wasn't Aunt Mary's assistant, she could easily get a job modeling. She is naturally beautiful and requires no makeup, but she is all business. Rarely do you see a different side to her.

"How is Felicia?" I ask Aunt Mary.

Aunt Mary lets out a long, exasperated sigh while running a hand through her thick mound of hair. "Felicia's having a hard time."

I remember this summer, Dee drew an interesting picture with stick figures of her father getting arrested. She drew other stick figures she described as her family with tears spewing from their eyes.

"Did you contact her father?" I ask.

"We sent a message. He's still in county jail. Who knows what happens at this point?" she answers.

"I can't imagine being in jail and getting news like that," Cassandra says.

"It's tough." Aunt Mary pours herself a glass of red wine before sitting on the sofa. Her assistant Leah sits nearby in an armchair, her long legs crossed, with a notepad resting on her lap.

"I stopped by Rosie's house. Her mother said she moved out about a month ago. Did you know this?" Aunt Mary asks me.

I pretend it's news to me. "Wow. I had no clue."

"Her mother told me she was staying with her boyfriend."

I continue my act.

"What do you do?" Cassandra asks her mother.

"Right now, I'm too exhausted to be Superwoman. Being around Felicia has zapped all my energy." Aunt Mary's expression grows pensive. "It's so unnatural to lose a child."

Cassandra joins her mother on the sofa and wraps her arms around her. Aunt Mary sets her glass of wine on the coffee table and returns the love with a tight squeeze.

"Felicia will never know the feeling of watching Dee grow into a beautiful young lady. I'm so grateful I have you." She kisses Cassandra's forehead. I notice her eyes glisten with tears.

Watching them makes me long for my mother. Aunt Mary must read my thoughts because she beckons me to join her and Cassandra.

"I'm grateful you gave me the opportunity to mother you. I could never be Evelyn, but my love is close enough," she says.

"How do you think Mother feels about me right now?" I ask.

My head rests on her right side. I hear her take a deep breath. "She wouldn't think any less of you. Her compassionate spirit would outweigh any shame or disappointment."

Hearing it is one thing, but what I wouldn't do to experience it.

"Mom, it's unfortunate what happened to the youth center, but I'm glad we'll have you around more," Cassandra says.

"I've got to be present. It's your senior year. We've got the debutante ball, senior pictures, the senior field trip, senior prom, graduation."

I remember the time and care Aunt Mary took getting me ready for my debut last year and how proud Daddy was presenting me. That seemed like a different time. It was back when I was certain I knew what the future held for me.

Sitting there, I'm lost in thought, feeling guilty for letting down my family. I ask myself constantly, *Is this pregnancy really happening?* I replay over and over what I would have done differently with JB. But it's hard because each time I think of him, I get butterflies.

"You're quiet, Maddie." I hear my aunt's voice, snapping me out of my thoughts.

I want to yell out, *I'm not ready. I don't want to go through with this pregnancy. I can read all the pregnancy manuals, and I still don't believe I'm capable of being a parent. I see Felicia without her daughter; I see myself without my mother. I don't want my child to experience that kind of loss. I don't think I could handle another loss.*

# Six

"He said he's coming," I tell Daddy and Aunt Mary. We're sitting inside a private waiting area at the doctor's office. Last night, JB and I talked, and he told me he was coming even if it meant missing part of his class. My appointment was scheduled for 10:45. It's 11:02, and the nurse has just called my name.

"We're waiting for someone. Give us a few minutes, please," I say to the nurse. Her smile is gracious, but I can sense she's growing a little impatient.

"Maybe he's still in class," Aunt Mary says.

"But he said he would be here," I answer.

"If he's in class, we need to proceed. Your physician's time is valuable. You're not her only patient," Daddy says to me.

"But I don't want to do this without him," I insist.

"We'll give him ten more minutes," Daddy says to the nurse. She nods and leaves the room.

I'm trying to manage my nausea. I thought it would be gone by now, but it lingers, appearing during morning hours and sometimes into late afternoon. I'm eating saltines, I'm drinking ginger ale. Sleep is my only comfort, and when I awake, I'm reminded of the life that's inside me. Again, I ask myself, *Is this real?* I cry sometimes, then I hear the clear voice of my conscious telling me in what sounds like my mother's voice, *I didn't raise you the first twelve years of your life to crumble at the first sign of a challenge.*

I don't understand myself how I'm supposed to mother a baby. I'm crying now.

Daddy takes my hand, and we pray, "Heavenly Father, whatever seeds of doubt and uncertainty that have taken root in the mind of my dear Madeline, I ask you to remove them, right now in the mighty name of Jesus, oh God. Put in their place, a spirit of peace. Give her courage and guide her in Your mighty son Jesus' name I pray. Amen."

Daddy taps my hand. "Wipe those tears." He reaches inside his coat to retrieve a handkerchief.

"I haven't felt this way since Mother died," I say, wiping my tears.

"And what's that feeling?" Daddy asks.

"Overwhelmed," I answer.

"You know the baby can sense that," Daddy says.

"I know now."

"Take care of yourself. It's no longer you anymore."

Ten minutes pass, and the nurse appears again with a smile. "Are you ready now, Miss Richardson?" she asks.

I take a deep breath. Still no JB. "Yes, I am."

Daddy feels it's best Aunt Mary accompanies me. If a procedure requires the physician to be invasive, he feels it'll be more appropriate for a woman to be present. He notes, "You wouldn't want me in the room when you're getting your well-woman's exam."

No, I wouldn't.

The nurse introduces herself as Rachael. I tell her how sorry I am for having her wait. I really want JB present.

"I'm sure he has a pretty good explanation," Rachael says, sounding upbeat.

"How far is USC from here?" I ask.

"Forty-five minutes on a good day," she responds, "Is that where he's coming from?"

I sigh. "Yes."

"That's my alma mater, class of '84," she announces proudly.

"Nice. It's my aunt's, too. She'd kill me if I told her class year."

Rachael tells me to step on a scale. I don't want to know the number. Next, she takes my blood pressure. She tells me it's a little elevated, but I'm sure it has a lot to do with me stressing out over JB. She wants to know the date of my last period, then she gives me a cup. I'm instructed to urinate up to a certain level and leave it in the restroom. After that's finished, I follow her into an examination room where Aunt Mary awaits. I sit on the exam table and wait for the physician. I notice glossy brochures about pregnancy, charts with drawings of the female uterus, and a wall with a sea of baby pictures.

I glance at my watch, and there's still no JB.

"Maddie, I remember classes lasted longer on Thursdays," Aunt Mary announces.

"It's the first visit. He needs to be here."

"I know the first visit is always special, but there'll be other visits. Hopefully you can schedule them when he's not in class."

The nurse enters with a beautiful obstetrician who happens to be a woman with full, feathery hair that stops at her shoulders. She smiles and greets Aunt Mary with a hug.

"Soror, it's been too long," she says to Aunt Mary.

"I get it. You're busy. Your wall of babies is all the proof I need."

"You see. The last time I took a vacation, Ford was in office."

"Oh no." Aunt Mary chuckles.

The physician turns her attention to me. "Madeline, I'm Dr. Blue." We shake hands.

"Please, call me Maddie."

"Maddie, let's take a look," she says.

I lie back on the exam table and feel Rachael the nurse lift my blouse.

"Maddie, I read that you are a concert pianist," Dr. Blue begins.

"Yes. I perform classical music."

"Awesome. I came to appreciate classical music when I was in med school," she says. "Chopin and Mozart are my favorites."

"They're in my top five," I respond.

"Now, Maddie, I will apply ultrasound gel on your stomach," Dr. Blue says. "This will be cold to the touch."

I feel the cold gel on my belly, followed by the cold device on my stomach. I look at a monitor and see what looks like the inside of my womb, and I hear a series of sounds—quick wavelengths—then the sound of a heartbeat. It's real, and there is the baby, a tiny spot with a heartbeat.

"The heartrate is 155 beats per minute. That's normal," Dr. Blue says.

The tears come. I glance at Aunt Mary who wipes away a tear.

"The measurements are average, looks normal, certainly sounds normal," Dr. Blue says with a bright smile. "We will print this out." She presses a button, and the exact image that was on the screen is printed out and given to me. The very first picture of my baby. It's strange to say *my baby* now that I've seen and heard a heartbeat.

"Birthday will be March 21."

The nurse Rachael gives me a folder, and inside, it contains different brochures and pamphlets and recommended reading.

The doctor has various samples of prenatal vitamins to give me.

"Try and see which one works with your body. Call me directly if you have questions or concerns," she says. "I'll see you next month." She turns to Aunt Mary, "Soror, hopefully we can link up before Maddie's next visit."

"At the moment, my calendar is clear. Just pick a day that ends with 'Y,'" Aunt Mary replies before they embrace, and we walk out of the room to the area where Daddy awaits. Dr. Blue introduces herself to Daddy, and they exchange small talk before she's off to the next patient.

"How did it go?" he asks me.

I give him the printout of the image.

"Look at that," he says with awe. He points to the dot on the image. "God is so awesome. Even a human life starts out as a tiny seed."

"I think you have a sermon for Sunday morning," Aunt Mary says before pressing the down button on the elevator. As the elevator door opens, JB appears. He's sweating, and he looks flustered.

"Sorry. I was speeding and got stopped."

"We're just leaving," I say.

"I missed it?" he asks.

"Yes" is my response. I don't know whether to be happy he tried or upset he didn't allow himself enough time to get here. He steps back into the elevator with us.

"Hello, Mr. Richardson. Hello, Mrs. Mary." He nods. Sweat beads pour down each side of his face. His soft, curly hair is a wet hive of ringlets.

"I'm sorry," he says to me.

"Were you issued a citation?" Daddy asks.

"Just a warning after I agreed to sign my autograph."

"I see," Daddy says.

Once the elevator door opens, we step into a busy waiting area. I forgot there was a private entrance and exit.

"We're just about to have lunch. Come join us," Daddy says to JB.

"Sounds good."

"Leave your car here and ride with us," Aunt Mary insists.

On the ride over, I show JB the printout of the ultrasound. He studies it for a long time, blinking as if he can't believe his eyes.

"It's really happening." He holds it.

"I know."

"In class, I couldn't concentrate. I kept watching the clock because I knew I had to be here at eleven o'clock."

"It was actually 10:45."

"That's when class ended. 'SC is huge. I'm rushing through the parking lot, almost ran over someone."

"No way," I hear Daddy respond.

"I weaved through traffic. Cop clocked me doing forty-eight in a thirty-five mile-per-hour zone."

I notice cops out here are relentless. It seems they stop you just because they can.

"The entire time this is happening, I'm thinking I've got to get to Maddie." He sighs. "And I'm late anyway."

I didn't want to give him a hard time for not showing up, but I wished he could've been there to see what I saw.

We look through my folder at the baby brochures and how-to pamphlets. I see a brochure that details what to expect from month to month, and there is also a place for me to write down my thoughts. He notices all the prenatal vitamins.

"When are you due?" he asks.

"March 21."

"When do you find out if it's a boy or girl?"

"If I remember reading correctly, it says around the twentieth week."

"Our last regular game is March 10. If we make it to March Madness, the season won't be over until April," he says while flipping through a brochure. A picture of a beautiful black baby captures his attention. Thoughts of him holding a baby run through my mind. The same attentiveness he's giving this image will be the exact same way he looks at our baby. I already hear him singing cute little songs and kissing the baby's feet. I imagine he'll be a good daddy.

During lunch, while eating, I notice a couple with a toddler sitting at a table across from ours. I observe the mother feeding the toddler, and the toddler makes the cutest face, showing a row of tiny teeth.

"That's going to be you and JB a year and a half from now," Aunt Mary says.

We both laugh in a nervous kind of way.

"I'm still trying to come to terms with this," Daddy says. "I've always pictured my only daughter—world-renown classical concert pianist—traveling constantly. No time for family. No time for a relationship. Just a girl doing what she loves. I never imagined this."

"Are you worried how the church will perceive you?" Aunt Mary asks.

"Not at all," he responds. "Maddie's well-being is my only concern."

"And how are you, Maddie?" Aunt Mary asks.

Before she opened the youth center, she had a clinic and practiced as a child psychiatrist. Her tone suggests she wants me to tell the truth and don't hold back.

"I'm not okay" is my response. I glance at Daddy for his reaction.

"Let's talk about it," Aunt Mary says.

"We've talked, and everything's pretty much already decided, and that's the part I'm not okay with."

"What's been decided?" she asks.

"Having this baby."

"How do you feel?" she asks JB.

"I feel like I've got a lot to prove. I can't let my personal circumstances affect my drive or my ambition," he declares.

I'm not there yet. Must be my pregnancy hormones. They have my thoughts vacillating between a girl who detoured on the road to her dreams who sits wallowing in her pain. On the other hand, I am the same girl reading pregnancy manuals and glossy brochures who approaches a mirror, hikes up her shirt, turns sideways, and examines the shape of her belly. I am a catastrophic composition—a cluster of notes with no clear distinction. Then I remember Aunt Mary's words to me and JB: *Don't get scared, get prepared.* No longer can I look at myself as naïve and seventeen.

*What do I do?*

I remember JB telling Aunt Mary that he stopped looking at me like a girl and started looking at me like a woman.

*I woman up. How do I do that?* I'll figure it out.

# Seven

I look up, and the sky is a shade of the deepest blue. Contrast it with the greenery of a well-kept cemetery and the gray defining various shapes of headstones. A large crowd gathers around a tiny gold casket surrounded by flowers and funeral wreaths. I stand next to JB. We hold hands, and in the distance, an official vehicle coasts up the gravel driveway. It stops, and minutes pass before the doors finally open. The driver, a law enforcement officer, gets out and opens the back door.

A man dressed in an orange jumpsuit is helped from the car. His hands and feet are bound in chains. He's escorted by law enforcement officers on each side. When the others in the crowd see them approaching, they part to make a way for him to view the casket. At the sight of it, his knees buckle, and the officers hold him up. They don't give him the luxury to mourn how he wants. He makes eye contact with Felicia, and I notice she sobs in her hands, her shoulders shaking uncontrollably with grief.

"That's the daddy," I hear someone whisper.

He stands before the closed casket, shaking his head. He says something. I feel bad for him. I don't know what he did to get locked up, but he was incarcerated the entire time Dee was ill. I rest my head on JB's arm.

"You want to sit?" JB asks.

"I'm fine."

"Aren't you worried about your feet swelling?"

I'm wearing a pair of wedge slingbacks, not ideal for a graveside service. Seating is limited. I see Aunt Mary is present along with Miss Vanessa, one of the teachers from the youth center. They both express kind words about Dee. Blaze, who was a student at the youth center, is here. My heart is heavy when I think of his friend, Damon. He lost a leg when a stray bullet hit it while he was playing outside at the youth center. Raquel, another one of the children from the youth center, sings Dee's favorite song, "The Greatest Love of All."

After the service, they surround me with hugs. All the memories of volunteering and teaching them piano overwhelm me, and I get emotional. There is still one person missing, and that's Rosie. I hope she's okay.

***

JB pulls into the driveway of his family's home. I hope his father isn't there. I get the sense he feels my pregnancy is intentional. Once inside, JB and I follow an aroma of garlic and butter into the kitchen. There, his mother pokes at something inside the oven. She has no idea we are in the room. She's babbling in a foreign language with the handset of the phone resting on her shoulder. JB taps her shoulder. I notice she jumps as he startles her. She continues to ramble in her language. He points her in my direction.

"Hi," she says with enthusiasm. Closing the oven, she walks up and gives me a warm hug. "Pretty little thing you are. You're just in time for class."

"Class?"

"Wash your hands and grab an apron," she tells me.

*Wash my hands, grab an apron?* I look at JB.

"Do what she says" is his reply.

I wash my hands and dry them off and watch her multi-task,

talking on the phone, stirring in a pot on the stove, and opening a kitchen drawer to retrieve an apron.

"What is going on?" I ask JB. "Did you bring me here to cook?"

"No, but you don't know how. I think today is a good day to start," he says, sitting on a barstool at the kitchen island. I did not see this coming. Judy hangs up the phone.

"Do you mind?" I ask her before slipping off my slingbacks and placing them off to the side.

"Not at all. You're in for a treat. I'm making Filipino ribs," she says. "I need you to help me prep. Can you do that?"

"Sure," I say aloud, but the surprise expression on my face reads otherwise.

I notice three onions, a bottle of soy sauce, and vegetable oil. JB pulls out a stool for me. I sit and watch her place a cutting board before me. She sets two onions on top of it.

"Basic food prep involves dicing. You do know how to dice an onion?" she asks.

"I've watched other people," I reply.

"There's really nothing to it." She grabs a knife.

"Okay."

First, she cuts the ends, next she cuts it in half before removing the outer layers.

"I started cooking when I was ten," she says. "My nanay worked all day, so she left me in charge of my brothers and sisters."

"Ten years old. Wow." I glance at JB.

The phone rings. "I'll be back," JB says, getting up. He looks nice in a suit wearing shiny black leather lace-up shoes. He captured the attention of so many people at the cemetery. I had no idea how popular he was. After the service, people who follow him in basketball were asking for his autograph.

"How are you?" Judy asks once we're alone. "Really, how are you?"

"I don't know" is my answer.

She nods in a sympathetic way. I watch her dice an onion half into perfect tiny squares. "I'm just kidding about prepping. You don't have to do anything. Relax."

I feel a sense of relief. I can work a Steinway, but knives intimidate me.

"Your uncle Frenchy sometimes flew the charters for the team. All the guys gravitated to him because it wasn't every day they saw a Black pilot."

"Uncle Frenchy's a cool guy."

"I told James if JB decides to marry you, he will marry well because your family is a class act."

I don't quite know how to respond.

"I'm told you play the piano," she begins.

"I started when I was nine. I never learned how to cook or babysit because my mom kept me practicing—always making sure I was ready for my next performance."

"I put JB in piano when he was eleven. It didn't last. His father took him out and made him focus on basketball."

"For someone who didn't spend a great deal of time learning piano, he plays really well."

"He's a quick study" is her reply.

"It's amazing how he can hear all the notes in a song and play them. Not me. I need to see the sheet music."

"He's gifted. He gets it from his father's side." She picks up a root and sniffs it. "Ginger root, good for nausea. You still have morning sickness?" she asks.

"I do."

She takes the ginger root and peels the outer layer with a tablespoon before she grates it.

"I make an awesome tea. We call it Salabat. You drink it in the morning. It won't hurt the baby." She stops and places a hand on my stomach "I know that's my grandbaby. I don't care what James says."

"When are we supposed to take the paternity test?" I ask.

"I don't know," she answers. "Seems ridiculous." She scoops up a handful of onions and drops them into the pot.

"Once we take the test, how long does it take to get the results?"

"I don't know, honey," she answers.

"May I ask you something?" I begin.

"Sure."

"Am I the only girl who's been with JB and gotten pregnant?"

She thinks for a minute. My heart has a sinking feeling.

"You are," she answers. "James has always drilled it in my son's head to be careful. Always use protection. Why he didn't with you—" She shrugs.

I watch her dice the other half of the onion, scoop it with her hands, and drop it in the pot. The pungent aroma of the onions has us both tearing.

"Believe me, I wasn't trying."

"You don't strike me as that kind. I look at you, and I see a girl who allowed my son to charm the panties off her."

I'm blushing at Judy's candid remark.

"I know I'm right. My son is a charmer. Always has been. Were you a virgin?" she asks.

I am surprised by Judy's direct question.

"I was," I answer.

"I knew it," she responds.

"How do you know?"

"You're different from the other girls he's been with. You're quiet, demure. You're a good girl."

"I see."

"I want to be candid with you," she begins.

"Sure."

"Babies sometimes bring people closer, and sometimes they drive a wedge between them. Just realize a baby doesn't stop the ball from bouncing in a basketball player's court."

"Okay." I'm following.

"Basketball will always come first."

I recall a conversation JB and I had about basketball being his wife and music his lover.

"In this world, the phone rings constantly: pro scouts, sports agents, newspapers, ESPN, old girlfriends, relatives wanting hand-outs. I was always second to basketball, but I understood my role."

JB enters wearing a USC basketball shirt with jeans and slip-on sandals. His hair is wet and curly from having just taken a shower.

"How did she do?" he asks.

"She's a quick study." She winks at me.

"Is homemaking class dismissed? I want to borrow the student for a minute," he says to his mother.

"What do you plan to do?" Judy asks. She pours a bottle of soy sauce into the pot and follows it up with brown sugar.

"Music class is starting," he says, taking my hand. "I've got a song I want you to hear."

I glance at Judy to make sure everything is finished with us.

"We'll talk later," she says.

"At some point, I want to shower and change out of this dress and get comfortable," I say to JB as he leads me to the pool house.

Smitty, the family's dog, leaps to his feet and rushes JB, happily wagging his tail. I kneel to pet and rub his coat. He returns the love by licking the side of my face.

"Chill, Smitty," JB says. "That's my job."

Inside the pool house, he flips on the light switch and turns on the stereo. He puts a tape into the player and pushes play. An intro with a slow yet jazzy tempo of horns, trumpets, and saxophones punctuated with a groovy organ sets a very romantic mood. I recognize Prince's falsetto. He's only one of a handful of popular voices I listen to. I wash my hands and dry them before JB sits on the bench in front of the keyboard and pulls me in for a long, tight hug. We don't say anything, but I sense he has a lot on his mind between my pregnancy, Dee's death, and whatever decision he makes regarding basketball. I sit on his thigh. We kiss, slow and tender. With his lips pressed against mine, he sings the lyrics to "Adore." I close my eyes while I twirl his ringlets around my fingers.

"You own my heart. You own my mind," he declares.

"Is that your way of saying you love me?" I ask, not sure what to expect.

"Yes," he answers.

"You do?" *Did I hear correctly?*

"I love you, Maddie." He looks into my eyes when he says it.

"How do you know?"

"Can you recall the last time we were together?" he asks.

"Together? Like intimate?"

"Yes."

I think for a minute. "Over a week ago."

"You know the last time I went this long without any?" he asks.

"No."

"Never," he says. "I never went this long."

"What does that have to do with loving me?"

"I care about you so much that I haven't been with anybody else," he declares.

I want JB. Truthfully, I have always wanted JB, even during times when I was with Gregory. There's something alluring about him. The song ends.

"What do you think?"

"I like it, of course. I actually like Prince's music."

"The lyrics are dope."

The phone rings, startling us. He moves me aside so he can get up to answer it. As he's talking, I pick up his worn, black-and-while speckled, composition notebook to read more songs: *It's in her walk. Her walk says everything. Her style, her flow. The confidence she brings.* I turn a page and read: *I dreamed of you—holding and kissing you, feeling you inside. You're warm and soft, I'm hard as steel, there's no limit to the way you make me feel. My dream is to love you. No other girl can fulfill my need, only you satisfy me.* I glance at him still on the phone. I read more lyrics:

*A song for her plays on the stage. The greatest sound of work for the ages. Sounds soar high into the rafters—fade into waning whispers, joys, and laughter. She prayed for a symphony but got the blues. Tired of promises not kept and baseless words of I love you. Alone she goes, into the world she goes, and where she ends, only she knows.* I don't know why reading this makes me sad—why between all the declarations of love and beauty, he writes this. What does it mean?

He hangs up and sits next to me. "I see you've been reading my songs."

"I'm curious, though. 'A Song for Her'—what is it about?"

He turns on the keyboard and plays chords. "It's about a girl who's lost her dream but eventually finds it."

"And who is this girl?" I ask.

"She's the one who identifies with the song" is his answer.

"If I didn't know you and I picked up this notebook and read these lyrics, I'd say you had an obsession."

"Obsession? No. Now, inspiration is more like it."

"You inspire me, too. I love you, JB," I say, feeling so emotionally overwhelmed that I can barely contain myself.

He cups my face in his hands and brings me in for a kiss. "I love you, too," he whispers against my lips.

"I won't stop loving you," I whisper back.

"I know. I feel it," he says.

The phone rings again as we kiss, and he breaks away again to answer it. His mother was right. I hear JB telling someone, "Okay, okay. I'll be there," he says before hanging up.

"You gotta go?" I ask.

"That was Pops. We're meeting with an agent."

"Okay."

He notices the twisted expression on my face. I'm a little disappointed that our quiet time has ended.

"You cool?"

"Yes."

Judging from his expression, he's not buying it.

"Listen, Maddie, if you want to take this crazy ride with me, this is what you deal with."

"Okay," I finally say after seconds of silence.

"You can stay here and eat ribs with Moms, or I can take you home."

I stay with Judy.

# Eight

I don't see or hear from JB again until the following Thursday. Meanwhile, I'm working with L.A. Phil on a couple of upcoming concerts. I'll be a guest pianist performing both piano and organ. Members of L.A. Phil welcome me; a couple musicians even remind me of the fall that happened after my performance. I tell them I was nervous and dehydrated. I will never tell them the truth. I'm managing the nausea thanks to the tea Judy made for me last Saturday. This house is quiet now that Cassandra and Caleb are in school. Aunt Mary is traveling to China with Uncle Frenchy on a flight he's piloting. Aunt Teal—Uncle Frenchy's older sister who's lived with the family since Caleb and Cassandra were small—sits upstairs in her room. She spends her days completing word search puzzles with the television on a soap opera. I read books on what to expect during pregnancy that Gilda mailed me.

I'm entering my eleventh week. Turning sideways, I examine my stomach and see a growing pooch. Do I start purchasing maternity clothes or just buy bigger sizes? I've always had enormous breasts—seems like they've gotten bigger. My areolas are tender to my touch.

When I see JB again, I'm fuming.

"Is this how it goes? We don't speak for days at a time?"

He glares at me. "What are you talking about?"

"You don't pick up the phone to call me."

"I'm crazy busy."

"Too busy to call me?"

"I guess I am" is his reply. His nonchalant attitude stings a little.

"Wow." *There it is.*

"Are you good?" he asks after a moment of silence.

"No." Tears blur my eyes.

He notices the tears. We are quiet the rest of the drive until we arrive at the facility.

JB's father, James, had already taken care of the financial part of the prenatal paternity testing. All JB and I do is show up. From what I gather, many celebrities use this location obviously because of its privacy protocols and because testing the paternity of the fetus can be done in a non-invasive way, anywhere from eight weeks to just prior to birth. Neither one of us can stand the sight of needles, so I turn my head when we both get our blood drawn. Next, they slap on Band-Aids and tell us to expect the results of the paternity test in two to three weeks. The quick turn-around is probably another reason why celebrities use this place. We are silent on the walk back to the car and for most of the ride.

"Tonight, my frat's hosting a party on campus. You're invited—get a glimpse of what it's like in my world."

"Party on a college campus? I've never been to one."

"Never?"

"No."

"One of the reasons I love you. I want to be the one you experience all your firsts with." He kisses me. Like that, every inch of my body comes alive. Now, I don't care if it's been five days since our last kiss. I close my eyes and relax because right now, at this very moment, I. Just. Want. To. Feel. Good.

After he drops me off, I call to invite Ursula to come along. She says she'll pick us up on the way. I tell Cassandra about it, and she immediately goes to her closet to find something. Hours later, when Ursula arrives, I tell Aunt Teal we're going out to eat. Ursula knows exactly where the party is. The campus is beautiful, like an oasis with Romanesque buildings, water fountains, and gorgeous people—like the people you see in movies or on the covers of *Seventeen* magazine. We follow a dense crowd to the sounds of loud bass thumping. We enter a building where the music intensifies, and the crowd is now shoulder to shoulder. Colorful lights dance and reflect off the walls. I see bodies of all shades dancing as I zigzag through the crowd. I see guys dressed in purple and gold spin on their heels and bark like dogs. Girls wearing the colors of my mother and Gilda's sorority yell in high-pitch squeals, flip luxurious manes of hair with choreographed hand and feet movements. I spot JB and Caleb dressed in jeans and polo shirts sporting their fraternity's letters. They are in a line. Their movements are synchronized, their attitudes are cocky —or confident depending on how you view it. I lose Ursula and Cassandra as I stand in the middle of the dense crowd, mesmerized. There must've been fifty of them in a line, arranged from the shortest to the tallest, ending with Caleb and JB.

I notice guys with no shirts, only sporting bow ties, their arms, chests, and backs branded with letters and symbols. Each guy has a candy-striped walking cane. They perform a routine—one that has them tossing their canes simultaneously in the air before they land with one unified sound. They break up into smaller groups and toss canes, twirling, stomping, chanting. The place cheers them on. The deejay switches to another song with an upbeat tempo, and JB separates from the line. He and the other guys with him disperse and go in different directions. JB now dances solo. I'm about to walk over when two girls surround him. I stop in my tracks. One dances in front of him while another clings behind, holding him close. He spins around and takes her hand, and they dance, not too close but arm's length until she draws him in and wraps her arms around him. In a rhythmic way, she seductively winds down to the floor. JB smiles, appearing to enjoy her sinuous movement.

"Don't just stand there. Ask me to dance." I glance in the direction of the voice and see a cute, muscular guy wearing purple and gold addressing me.

"I'm here with someone," I yell over the music.

"And he left you alone?" he asks.

I flip my hair and run a hand over the front of my saffron-colored, off-the-shoulder mini dress. It was the only stretchable fabric I could find. At eleven weeks with a small pooch, I still have a slim waist. I have hips and a round butt with ample, overflowing breasts. I don't want to seem impolite. I wish Ursula were here so she could entertain him instead. I glance in the direction where I saw JB last, and he's gone.

"Excuse me," I politely tell the guy and meander through the thicket of dancers. I hear conversations, squeals, dogs barking, cats meowing. I get caught up in the middle of a couple dancing. I hurry and move aside. I see Caleb and people gathered around him. I move on until I spot JB. He, too, is surrounded, and I stroll over and make my presence known. In this dark room with dancing lights, I catch his eye. The people around him follow his gaze. With the flip of my hair, I approach, walking in my way that drives him crazy. He even wrote about it in his notebook. I imagine how I must look to him. He brushes past the group to meet me. It feels like a dream sequence in a movie where everything else becomes a blur. Only JB and I are in focus.

"You look incredible," he whispers in my ear.

"Thank you," I respond.

"Did you just get here?" he asks.

"Yes."

Our conversation is interrupted by people stopping to say hello to JB. A fraternity brother dressed in full regalia starts chanting, and before long JB forgets about us and starts chanting with him. Soon, a group of his brothers join, chanting and singing. Caleb comes over to chant and sing. He sees me and frowns as if he can't believe his eyes. He beckons me to step away from the gathering to a place where we can talk.

"What up?" he asks.

"Hi, Caleb."

"You see how it goes down at 'SC?" he asks.

"Yes."

"It's like this every week."

"No way." As we're talking, I'm observing the room, and I admit, I can't keep my eyes off JB.

"So, Wolf got you in?"

"No. Ursula."

"Ursula?" He glances around the room. My guess is he's hoping to catch a glimpse of her for whatever reason.

"Yes. She knows where all the good parties are."

As we talk, people approach Caleb. He slaps high fives and banters with them. *It's nice to be well-known.*

"We'll talk later," he says, walking off into another direction just as Cassandra approaches me from behind.

"You just missed your brother," I say to her.

"I'm not trying to run into him."

I notice a red cup in her hand.

"What are you drinking?"

"You can't have it," she says to me.

"Why? What is it?"

"It's 7-Up."

"And what else?"

"Just 7-Up."

I can already see her eyes are glassy.

"You're wasted."

"No, I'm not." She frowns before taking another sip

"Where's Ursula?" I ask.

"She grabbed a frat boy and split."

"No, she did not." My heart is racing.

"I don't know if she left campus—she might be in a dorm room."

"She needs to stop."

"Or she'll end up pregnant like her friend?"

Cassandra's remark has a sting to it.

"No. Something worst, like HIV," I respond. "Do you know who she left with?"

"He's JB's and Caleb's frat brother. I know because he's wearing the letters."

I felt somewhat at ease. Someone catches Cassandra's eye.

"He's so fine. Omigod, I'm looking forward to this next year."

"Did you forget about Kyle?"

"No crime in looking and admiring."

"Seriously, whatever's in that cup, I suggest you pour it out."

"I'm done talking. Now there's a spot on the dance floor with my name on it."

She strolls through the crowd, snapping her fingers while holding on to her drink. I'm now alone in this crowded place. I don't recognize the song playing, and JB has since moved from the spot where I saw him last. I find a chair to sit, cross my legs and observe. Girls from a different sorority—the one that Aunt Mary belongs to—gather to pose for a picture. Two girls in the center, one uses her right hand, the other uses her left hand to form a pyramid. They make *Ooo-op* sounds.

I find college black Greek culture fascinating. Whatever song is playing, they have a choreographed routine to go with it, punctuated with chants and calls. The deejay announces the next twenty minutes is dedicated to the lovers, so he plays slow melodies. Couples get close and slow dance. I notice Paul behind the lens of a handheld camera, capturing every moment. He pans the room and aims the camera in my direction. He makes his way over. Starting at my feet, he pans upward with the camera stopping at my face. He looks from behind the lens.

"Damn" is all he says.

"Paul," I yell.

He's shocked I know his name. "Have we met?" he yells back.

"Yes. I'm Maddie, Caleb's cousin."

He thinks about it for minute. "The pianist."

"Yes."

"You look different," he says. "Why aren't you out there dancing?"

"I don't want to."

"Then why are you here?"

"You sure ask a lot of questions."

"I'm trying to understand why someone as beautiful and fine as yourself is sitting here alone."

"Not anymore. You're here."

"Well." He's blushing as he glances at his camera. Paul has small beady eyes and a dimpled chin. He wears round-frame glasses that make him look geeky. He pulls up a chair and sits next to me.

"I bet you sleep with that camera," I say.

He pushes his glasses over his nose, reminding me of Gregory. "Sometimes."

"Is that why they call you Hollywood?"

"Yeah," he responds.

"You still have the video of me playing 'Rhapsody in Blue'?"

"I have video of you?"

"Yes. You don't remember?"

"I have so many. I would've remembered yours, though."

"Well, you do have a video of me playing "Rhapsody in Blue." Now, what are you going to do with it?"

"I don't know yet. I might do a documentary."

"What's your major?" I ask.

"Cinematic arts," he answers.

"You want to make movies and documentaries?"

"That's the plan."

Instantly, I feel envy. He's in school doing what he loves, and he doesn't have to worry about anyone but himself. How I wish I were at Juilliard.

"You want to go somewhere quiet and talk?" he asks.

"Actually, I'm waiting for someone," I tell him.

"I hope they don't keep you waiting long." He stands and puts the camera over his eye. "I'll see you around."

The deejay segues to another slow song. It's "I Need Love" by LL Cool J. I'll always remember where I was the first time I heard it. I get up and move from my spot to walk to another section of the room. Mostly everyone knows the song verbatim. There are moments when the deejay stops the record and the crowd finishes the lyrics. Walking through the dense crowd, I feel someone grab my hand. I look, and it's JB. He pulls me in close and whispers in my ear, "I need love."

It's hard to embrace him initially. I feel he's been ignoring me all this time, but I put my arms around him anyway. I move my hands up and down his back where I feel firm, tight, athletic muscle.

"Let's go," he whispers.

I admit, I like it when he takes my hand and guides me to wherever he wants me to go. We move through the crowd until we're outside where the night air is cool—my guess, it's sixty-five degrees. I think about Ursula and Cassandra and whether I'll see them before the party ends.

"I'm worried about Ursula and Cassandra," I tell him. "I can't find them."

He glances at his watch. "I wouldn't sweat it."

"Easy for you to say. You're not the one with a curfew."

The campus is alive with parties and loud music coming from all directions. People approach us.

"J-Fucking-B, my man. Fight on." Guys wearing togas and Jesus sandals are loud and boisterous.

"Let's get a championship this year," another yells.

I'm hearing "fight on" from passersby. More people stop him and talk. JB happily engages them.

"You're pretty popular," I say once it appears the interruptions have ceased.

"Welcome to my world," he says.

I hear a band of trumpets, snare drums, and clashing cymbals echoing in the night air. Their blended sounds recall a theme song that ancient Romans and Greeks play before they go to battle.

"That's our fight song," he mentions to me. The song brings out a certain energy, like victory is always imminent. It gets the people we see walking on campus energized.

"You need to hear it on game day at the coliseum," JB says.

"It will definitely be a first for me," I say, remembering what JB said about firsts.

After pointing out buildings where he takes classes and the facility where he trains and plays basketball, we arrive at an apartment. Once he unlocks the door and we're inside, it has his odor of leather. It's cluttered. I see a pizza box on top of the counter and dishes in the sink. His walls are decorated with posters of athletes. I see his fraternity's letters, along with pictures of him with his fraternity brothers. I pick up a framed five-by-seven photo of him and his parents. He's center with James and Judy on each side. It reads: *Harvard Prep Class of 1985*. I see a poster with the word *INVICTUS* written in bold letters, and underneath it is a poem. On the coffee table, sports and nude girlie magazines are scattered about. He lights an incense and turns on the stereo.

"Where's your roommate?" I ask.

"At the party."

JB takes my hand, and we sit on the sofa. The lighting in the room is a deep, sensuous red. The song playing is the latest from Michael Jackson, "I Just Can't Stop Loving You."

I like how it starts with him talking and the synthesizer arrangement sounds like string instruments in the background.

The glare of the red light on JB's tan complexion makes him appear like an image out of a dream. I feel his eyes connect with mine. It's one of the things I love about him, how he looks at me without saying a word and I know exactly what he's thinking. His lips are like a suction against my cool skin. I love how his soft curls feel on the tips of my fingers.

"I've just set a record," he says.

"How?"

"Fifteen days. That's how long it's been for me."

We spend the next hour or so making up for the days missed.

# Nine

I set my alarm to wake Cassandra up for school. I shake her, slap her face, and pull back her eye mask. She grabs a pillow and tosses it at me.

"I'm not going," she mumbles into her pillow.

"Yes, you are."

"No."

"You don't want to be here when your parents arrive."

"They're not coming today."

"Yes, they are."

She mumbles incoherently before rising and stretching.

I leave her room and return to mine, where Ursula lies uncovered at the foot of the bed in a fetal position. I cover her with the duvet before I go downstairs. I smell bacon, and I find Aunt Teal in the kitchen whipping something in a bowl before pouring it over a griddle. I hear it sizzle.

"Good morning." I give her a hug.

"Good morning, chère. How was dinner last night?"

"It was fun. We met up with more friends," I lie.

"What did you eat?"

"Italian."

She flips the pancake to the opposite side to cook. I notice fresh-cut melon, berries, bacon slices, and fresh-squeezed orange juice.

"How are you feeling?" she asks.

"So far, good," I answer. "I should be asking you. You're the one who does all the cooking."

"Mary acts like she forgot how to." She scoops the pancake with the spatula and slides it onto a plate and sets it in front of me. "I can't tell you the last time she stood in front of this stove."

I say grace quietly before eating.

"I'm moving back home to New Orleans when Cassandra graduates," Aunt Teal announces.

"Oh no." I'm chewing.

"Yes. It's time," she says.

"What are we going to do without you?"

"Bebby, you all will figure it out." She pours more pancake batter onto the griddle.

"You can't go back, Aunt Teal."

"I put in twenty years. That's long enough."

Moments later, Cassandra enters. She gives Aunt Teal a hug and sits next to me. She's dressed in a school uniform with loafers. Her hair is pulled back into a ponytail.

"Did you know Aunt Teal's moving back?"

"She's been saying it for years." Cassandra forks slices of melon and strawberries.

"I'm for real this time."

"Why? Don't you like us anymore?" Cassandra asks.

"You want the truth, or do you want me to tell you what you want to hear?" Aunt Teal jokes.

"I'm not letting you leave." Cassandra forks a pancake onto her plate. "If you do, I'm coming with you."

"You wouldn't last a week in New Orleans," Aunt Teal says.

Even Cassandra finds the remark funny.

"You know I'm right," Aunt Teal replies.

"Tell me what's in New Orleans," Cassandra says.

"That's where our roots are, bebby."

"But everyone you know is dead or moved away."

"Not everyone."

"You can't move back. You'll have to stay here forever." Cassandra gives Aunt Teal a hug and a kiss before taking one last sip of her orange juice. She grabs her books and walks out the door. I finish my pancake and fruit before I go back upstairs to find Ursula's still asleep. My rehearsal with L.A. Phil isn't for another three hours, so I spend quiet time reading the score for an upcoming performance. I hear Ursula stir. She tosses and turns before finally sitting up. She looks around the room. She sees me and breathes a sigh of relief.

"You okay?" I ask.

She wipes sleep from her eyes and runs both hands through her hair. "I am now."

Then out of the blue, she asks, "Did I see you and JB leave his apartment last night?"

"You did," I admit. The secret is out.

"Really? Is this a one-time thing?" she asks.

"No."

"You guys are dating?"

"We are," I say.

"When did you start dating?"

I take a deep breath. "Recently."

"Does he know you're pregnant?"

"Yes."

It's like her mind is piecing things together. "Okay. So you broke up with Gregory to get with JB?"

It sounds messy when it's put into that perspective.

"JB's the father."

Her mouth drops. "No way."

"He's the father," I repeat.

"Maddie, that's wild," she says.

"My summer summed up in one word."

"Wow, you and JB?" Her expression reveals her shock.

"I know."

"I did not see that coming."

"We're in love."

Her mouth drops. "Are you serious?"

"I am."

"JB is a cool guy." It's like she's searching for words.

"He is."

"I'm sure he'll make a wonderful father," she stammers.

"He will."

"You guys will have a beautiful baby."

"Thank you."

"I hope the baby has your eyes." As she talks, I notice her studying them.

"It doesn't matter as long as it's healthy."

"Do you want a boy or a girl?"

"I don't care."

"I would want a girl. I'd dress her up every day." She places a hand on my stomach, "When does the baby start moving?"

"Around the sixteenth week."

"When will you know the sex of the baby?"

"During the twentieth week."

"How far along are you?" she asks.

"It's my eleventh week."

She starts counting. "Were you with JB and Gregory at the same time?"

I don't like to talk about myself, and this situation is messy, so talking about it to someone is a big deal.

"My first time was with JB. I didn't think Gregory was coming back from Europe."

"Didn't JB have a girlfriend?"

"They weren't together. When Gregory came back, JB and I stopped hooking up. I started hanging out with Gregory, and JB went back to his girlfriend."

"Well, you're prettier than her anyway," Ursula says, "and I'm not just saying it because you're my friend. It's true, even if you weren't."

"Thank you."

She rests a cheek in the palm of her hand. "I really thought you and Gregory were cute."

I sigh. "I liked Gregory, but then I realized I like JB a lot more." I look at the bracelet still on my hand. "Gregory gave me this. I wanted to give it back when we broke up, but he lost the screwdriver."

Ursula examines it. "You know what that means?"

"What?"

"You're linked to him. Forever."

"No, I am not. I want this off."

"You can use any small flathead," she says. "Gregory knew what he was doing when he purchased it." She laughs.

"I don't want any reminders of him."

"Are you sure you have him out of your system?" Ursula asks.

"I'm positive."

He's out of my system. If I accidentally run into him on the street, I'll be fine. Gregory is the past. Could we be friends? I don't know.

After a rehearsal that lasts four hours, I come home, eat dinner, and take a shower before I lie across the bed to open my journal. I notice the last entry was August 12. I grab a pen to start a new entry.

*Friday, September 4, 1987 9:52 p.m.*

*Prepping for Juilliard, I spent a year putting together an audition tape of me playing medleys of my favorite composers: Chopin, Bach, Brahms, Liszt, and Rachmaninoff. I wowed them with my audition. A month later,*

*I received an acceptance letter. It was an incredible moment. It was always my dream to do intense study with classical music and eventually compose a symphony. I still dream of hearing an orchestra play my music. I want some little girl or little boy to sit on the edge of their seat the way I used to and hear the heartfelt sounds of a viola or the rippling waves of a cello. There is nothing more beautiful than an orchestra of instruments playing music that started as an idea that eventually found its way on paper.*

*Now I'm with L.A. Phil. I'm excited they've got me as a guest pianist until November, which is good. Hopefully I'm not showing by then. I do feel self-conscious. I guess I don't want to face questionable stares and puzzling minds—she's so young, and where is her husband?*

*I find it very hard not to think about JB so much. I could be in the middle of studying a score and start daydreaming about us cuddled together. I remember the cool feel of his breath against the back of my neck. How did we fall so quickly? It's supposed to take time for love to develop. He says he loves me; he says he wants to be with me. He writes songs about me. He waits for me. I don't think he's playing. I think he's sincere. As I write this entry, my heart flutters, and it feels like the wind has rustled the wings of a thousand butterflies.*

Aunt Mary and Uncle Frenchy are back from China with souvenirs. Cassandra and I get Chinese-embroidered silk robes. My robe is exactly like the colors of USC, cardinal red with the gold embroidery. Cassandra's robe is royal blue and gold. Caleb gets a Chinese puzzle. It's now Saturday morning, and I can't remember the last time the entire family had breakfast together. Our conversation is stilted at times, and in the back of my mind I'm wondering, *What are they thinking?* After breakfast is done, I get a call, and it's JB.

"Let's take a ride," he says.

"Give me a couple of hours."

"A couple?"

"Yes."

I say a couple of hours because by the time he arrives, everyone except Aunt Teal will be gone. A little over two hours later, when I see his car pull into the driveway, I tell Aunt Teal that I'm going to rehearsals. I don't know what he has in store, but I have my backpack with toiletries and a change of clothes. When he gets out of the car to open the passenger's door for me, I notice he's dressed casually in a white cotton t-shirt paired with acid-wash denim shorts. I'm wearing an oversized yellow shirt with red stretchy leggings. Although I have a small pooch, I don't need to wear maternity clothing—yet.

"You're glowing," he says to me once we're inside the car.

"What does that mean?" I ask.

"Your skin's brighter; your eyes sparkle. I like it," he says with a smile.

"Thank you." I tuck a curl behind my ear. "Must be the prenatal vitamins."

He lets down the top, and we cruise the boulevard. He puts in a tape. "L.A. Dream Team for your ears. You wouldn't know nothin' about that."

I listen and ride and watch him bob to the rhythm. The song reminds me of the night Cassandra and I took Rosie, our friend from Aunt Mary's youth center, to Skateland in Compton. The keyboards, the programmed drums, the repetitious rhyme, like the record is scratching. JB is really into the music; his shoulders are moving. We're at a light, and he's caught the attention of others. He turns down the volume.

"I remember the parties we turned out with this jam," he sings.

"I saw you and Caleb the other night. Everyone was treating you guys like stars."

"That's right. Twinkle, twinkle baby." He winks.

"Caleb says 'SC is like one big party."

"He's right. You name it—frat parties, toga parties, darties, wine Wednesdays, game day tailgating, Halloween."

"Back up. What's darties?" I ask.

"Imagine it's one o'clock in the afternoon, and there's a party in your dorm room."

"Parties are too loud."

"The louder the better, I don't care—just give me room, and let me do my thing."

"You like being the center of attention?"

"I don't go out of my way to seek it, but if I have the spotlight, you're getting a show." He lifts his shirt and starts rolling his belly. It ripples like waves.

"Stop."

"You like it."

I'm smiling because I agree.

I don't ask where we're going. I've learned with JB to sit back and enjoy the ride. I put on my sunglasses and recline my seat. The mid-afternoon September breeze tickles the hairs on my arms while the sun kisses a spot on my forehead. The traffic is stop-and-go. JB shifts gears and maneuvers between lanes. The thought just occurred to me that I haven't been nauseous. It's going into my twelfth week, and from what I remember reading, a full pregnancy lasts forty weeks, and morning sickness could last from ninety to one hundred and twenty days. It was eighteen days ago when I first learned I was pregnant. For the past two days, I've felt fine.

We pull into the driveway of a white stucco structure with tall palms. The yard is neatly manicured with a bed of marigolds. I notice it's within walking distance of the ocean. I look at JB, anticipating his next move.

"Where are we?" I ask.

"I need your opinion," he says before getting out to the car. I open the passenger door, and I notice he has a key. We approach the door of the structure, and when he opens it, the smell of fresh paint fills my senses. I look around, and the place is empty. When it occurs to me what's happening, I smile. He nods.

"Take a look around. See if you like it," he says to me.

My heart is pounding to the point where it feels like it's pouring out of my ears. The ceiling is tall; a spiral staircase leads to a loft. We're standing in the living room, and to my delight it's big enough for a baby grand—maybe a sofa and a loveseat. From where we're standing, I can see a small, narrow kitchen. I won't be spending much time in there anyway. There is an area for a round dinner table and a sliding door leading to a fenced-in patio. I open the patio to check out the view. Not much to see other than the other neighbors' homes. I go back inside, and off the living room is a bedroom with a full bath. I'm already imagining a bedroom suit and the spot where the baby's crib will be.

He stands with his hands in pockets, waiting for my reaction.

"I like it."

"You do?" He seems surprised.

"It's my own space. That's all I want."

He nods. "One day I'll find you something much bigger."

I scan the room once more, reimagining the space already furnished.

"When can I move in?" I'm getting excited.

"I don't know. I think my frat's dad has it set up where you talk to a leasing agent."

"There's one problem: I'm not old enough."

"We'll work around that," he says.

"Really? How?"

"I'll handle it."

"Thank you," I say.

"For what?" He pulls me in close.

"For making this work."

He kisses my forehead. "That's what I'm supposed to do," he says.

# Ten

When I tell Aunt Mary and Uncle Frenchy that I've found a place and soon I'll be moving out, they are stunned silent. Days after seeing the townhouse, I bring Ursula along to meet the leasing agent and go over the details of the leasing agreement. Because she's nineteen, she can sign. JB can't—something about his scholarship and NCAA rules. Daddy wasn't signing, and he told me to forget about asking Gilda. He said he'll have no part in enabling a lifestyle counter to his Christian beliefs. Having my own space means no rules, and if JB wants to spend the night, my door is always open.

"Who signed your lease?" Uncle Frenchy asks.

"Ursula," I answer.

"My God" is his response.

"How long is the lease?" Aunt Mary asks.

"It's month-to-month."

"How much is rent?" Uncle Frenchy asks.

"It's twelve hundred," I answer.

"You say it's a townhouse?" he asks.

"Yes, in Santa Monica, and it's close to the beach."

"Hence the steep rent," he says, glancing at Aunt Mary.

"I thought the point of you staying in L.A. was for us to monitor your situation should anything out of the ordinary occur," Aunt Mary explains.

"And you can still do that. Santa Monica's only twenty minutes away."

"What does your father have to say?" Aunt Mary asks.

"He's not happy," I tell her.

"I hope you told him Mary and I had nothing to do with this," Uncle Frenchy adds.

"Daddy knows all of this is my idea. Now that I have my obligation with L.A. Phil, I can take care of myself."

"Congratulations on your working with L.A. Phil. We're so proud of you," Aunt Mary says.

"I'll be doing a lot of rehearsing, which reminds me: May I have the piano from the youth center?" I ask Aunt Mary after what seems like an eternity of silence.

"You plan to hire a piano moving company?" she asks.

"Yes," I answer.

"Do with it as you wish," she answers in a tone to suggest she's over me.

"I'm rarely at a loss for words," Uncle Frenchy begins.

I can tell my pregnancy, my relationship with JB, and my sudden decision to leave bothers him.

"If you can handle it, then live your life the way you see fit."

I tell Cassandra, and she looks sad.

"You can visit—help me watch the baby," I tell her.

"You have absolutely no freaking idea how weird that sounds," she says.

"I know."

"It's like the shooting. Something like that happens to other people; you don't think it happens to you."

"It does, but I can't think about it too much."

"I'll miss you," Cassandra says.

Though I'll be minutes across town, I'll be a world away. I count the days until I'm out. I'm packing, and between packing, I'm performing. I invite Aunt Mary, Uncle Frenchy, Cassandra, and Aunt Teal to a performance. The following night, I invite JB to a show. From my vantage point, I see him on the edge of his seat, totally engulfed in my performance of Bach's "Toccata and Fugue in D Minor." This time I'm not mastering the piano but capturing the experience on the organ. My performance lasts nine minutes, and when it's complete, I stand and bow to receive the thunderous applause of the audience. I see JB applaud; his smile is warm. After the show, he greets me with a small bouquet of roses.

"One word: incredible," he says. "I had no idea you play the organ too."

As we talk, other members of the orchestra stop and compliment my performance. I am surprised when a couple of the members ask for his autograph. I can't believe they follow sports. Walking to the car, squeezing his hand, I've never felt so close. I feel a warm, electric energy when I'm with him. Days later, when all my things, including the piano, are assembled and moved into the townhouse, we collapse on a queen-sized bed. We're both laughing.

"Can I stay with you tonight?" he asks in a sweet, soft, mellow way.

"Only if you agree to sing me a song."

"What do you want to hear?"

"I don't know. Make up something."

"Let's play something on the piano," he suggests.

A smile as wide as the coast flashes across my lips. It's a care-free feeling. It's freedom. I can get on my piano and play anytime I choose. I play my favorite, Chopin's "Prelude in E Minor."

JB starts to sing:

*I'm singing a love song*
*All day long*
*Because my feelings are so strong*

*I don't care who thinks it's wrong*
*With you is where I belong*

Sitting next to me, he goes on, improvising. I'm listening, follow-ing his tone and tempo. His voice complements the harmony. I'll never listen to the song in the same way now that he's put words to accompany the melody. When I stop playing, we laugh. It feels so good to laugh.

"Remember playing house when you were a kid?" he asks.

"Is that when you pretend to be adults and make mud pies?"

"Something like that."

"Are we playing house?" I ask.

He takes a minute before answering. "Yeah, we are."

His expression is dreamy, like he's thinking about something.

"What's for dinner?" I ask.

"I don't know. Why don't you make a mud pie?"

"You're so silly."

We're quiet and gazing into each other's eyes.

"I love you," he says.

"I love you too."

"You're easy to love," he says.

"I didn't think you would at first, but you surprised me," I say.

We kiss. It's soft and tender, and while kissing, I hear my stomach growl. Seconds later, his stomach growls, and it sounds like some-thing's inside trying to claw its way out. We're laughing, but I have nothing in the house to eat and nothing to eat it with. The phone line is dead, so we can't call and order delivery. We hop in the car and go to the nearest McDonald's. I haven't eaten at a McDonald's since I was a child, so I don't know what to order. JB pulls up to the drive-thru and orders Big Macs, fries, drinks, and apple pies. When he's given the total, he reaches inside his pocket for his wallet. He opens it, and he pulls out a twenty, and the rest of the wallet is empty.

"I've got it," I say, reaching inside my pochette.

"What did I tell you before we even started kicking it?" he asks.

"You've got me," I answer.

He nods. "Right. What does it mean?"

"You'll take care of me?" is my answer.

"Even if it means giving you my last dollar," he says.

"But aren't we a team?" I ask.

"Yes, but I've got this, okay?"

He pulls the car up to the window to pay for our food, and I nearly leap out of the front seat when I see who's standing there.

"Rosie," I scream.

She cranes her neck wondering who could possibly be screaming her name. When she recognizes me, her eyes light up, and her mouth is wide.

"Maddie," she squeals.

JB looks at me then looks at her. "You two know each other?" he asks.

"Yes," I say, feeling flushed with excitement. She's working at Mickey Ds, just like she told me she would this past summer when the youth center was open.

"You want to go inside?" he asks me once Rosie gives us our food and his change.

"Sure."

Inside, the McDonald's lobby is crowded. JB and I find a corner booth to sit. My heart races with excitement. Rosie comes over in her uniform. I read "Ro" on her name bar, and we embrace. I almost cry. She's wearing a visor with her ponytail pulled through the opening in the back. I last saw her two months ago, and there isn't a day that I'm not wondering about her. I introduce her to JB.

"Wow," she says. Her smile is wide and bright. "Hi."

JB waves and points to a seat.

"My break is short," she says, sitting next to me.

"How have you been?" I ask.

"Working."

I remember Rosie living in a neighborhood not far from the youth center. I want to ask why she chose here, but I'm sure she has her reasons. She's only fourteen. I hope for her sake no one here finds out.

"Mrs. Mary saw your mom and your mom told her."

"Told her what?" Her cheerful expression turns serious.

"That you moved in with Dante and his family."

"What did Mrs. Mary say?"

"Nothing."

"Really?" Rosie's expression goes from serious to blank, not quite sure if she should be concerned. I remember her telling me that she was removed from her mother's care once and placed in foster care. I can't imagine what that's like. I can't imagine it happening to her again. She glances at JB and smiles.

"My boyfriend likes the Trojans," she says.

"Me, too," JB responds with a wink before sipping from the straw.

Rosie's cheeks flush. It's wild how JB has that effect on the people he meets, especially females.

"I've gotta go," she says.

"Hey, I just moved nearby," I say.

Okay" is her response. "I'm still in the J's."

"Really?" JB answers, and the look on his face clearly wants to know why she passed up at least twenty McDonald's to work at this one.

"Long story," she says.

When we embrace, her hugs are always warm and tight. She waves goodbye to JB and slides out of the booth, returning to her spot. She takes one last glance at us before resuming her duties.

"How old is she?" JB asks.

I bite into my Big Mac, chew, swallow, and sip my drink before finally answering. "Take one guess."

He shrugs. "She looks too young."

I don't want to say much about her, so I change the subject. "I've always wanted siblings, and when I met Rosie and Dee, they became my pretend little sisters," I tell JB. "Rosie is the artist who drew all the sketches for Dee. She even did that mural on Aunt Mary's building."

"This girl?" JB points.

"Yes."

"She painted that?"

"She said it took a month."

JB dips a fry in ketchup and bites. "Is she in school?" he asks.

"I don't know."

"Too bad you don't have a phone. You could leave her a contact number," he says.

"I have no phone, no food in the refrigerator, no car."

"Can you drive a stick?" he asks.

"What do you think?"

"If you could drive as good as you ride, I'll give you the keys to my car," he says with a big grin.

I'm trying not to laugh out loud. When we finish eating, I borrow a pen and grab a napkin to write down my address. I get Rosie's attention and place it in her hand.

"Don't lose it," I tell her.

"I won't," she says.

I leave thinking, *How will she get home?* then I remember Rosie is not the average fourteen-year-old. She didn't grow up with a charmed, sheltered life. She had already been through foster care. I even imagine she's already had sex. I can't stop the tears from flowing. I hide them by staring out the window at the darkness and the fog that's creeping in off the ocean.

"I should've asked what time she gets off."

"If she lives in the J's, why is she in Santa Monica?" JB asks.

"Next time, I'll ask."

We stop at Vons supermarket to pick up the basics: bread, slices of deli meat, and a carton of orange juice. I was so excited to be finally getting a place that I didn't take in consideration I needed a phone; pots and pans; knives, spoons and forks; plates; toilet paper; paper towels; bath soap; bath towels; and washcloths. I need laundry detergent and a washer and dryer. The townhouse doesn't have one, and I may for the first time ever have to wash at a laundromat or pay a dry-cleaning service to wash for me. I can't crawl back to Aunt Mary and Uncle Frenchy, and I refuse to fly back to Houston to Daddy. We come back to the townhouse to sit at the piano, and I show JB piano basics: reading notes, measure lines, timing, rhythm, and when to rest between notes. I teach him how to read sharps, flats, naturals, and keys. He is so eager to learn.

"I'm always hearing music. I wish I could write it down," he says to me. "It gets lost. I need you to help me."

I'm gazing at his face. It's so easy to get caught up in his looks and the laid-back feel of his energy. I forget this is supposed to be a teaching moment. Minutes later, his name echoes off the bare walls in the townhouse. I don't know what time it is when we finally rest. We cuddle, my back to his chest. I feel his heart slowly easing back to its normal rhythm. Now he's asleep. I'm constantly thinking, thinking about us: *How do I remain secure within when I'm with someone who constantly attracts attention wherever he goes? Do I consume myself with music and just ignore it?*

I'm thinking about Rosie and how coincidental it seems she works at a McDonald's that's blocks away from here. My thoughts drift to Aunt Mary and Uncle Frenchy and my decision to leave them. Aunt Mary sat me down and had a heart-to-heart with me. She said I could come to her anytime and talk. I think about all those girls and guys from the party at USC having fun. How I envy them. I should be happy with L.A. Phil. To some that is a dream-come-true position, so why do I still feel so empty—like it's still not enough?

\*\*\*

I awake to find JB gone. I scan the room in search of clothing or a note he might have left behind. I felt him stirring earlier, but I was too tired to move. I use the McDonald's cup from last night, pouring out watered-down soda and rinsing it to pour a cup of orange juice. I make a turkey sandwich with the deli meat before I walk outside to stand on the patio. The sky is foggy, gray, and hazy, and the roar of the city has ceased, at least for the moment. The fence protecting the patio is high so I can't see over it unless I get a chair to stand on. I notice a blue television light coming from the townhouse across the walkway. It flickers often. I go back inside and sit before the piano to practice a musical piece. I have a performance scheduled for tonight at eight. I unpacked most of my clothing, filling up the closet in my bedroom. Looking through my book of compositions, I see the pictures that Rosie drew. I thumb through more pages and see the picture Dee drew of me the very first time I met her. I remember her saying when she grows up, she wants to be pretty. Tears come, and soon sobs—loud, mournful sobs—the kind that are trapped and finally given a chance to be free. I work on my sunset composition until I am mentally exhausted.

Hours later, JB enters carrying a medium-sized box. He places it on the kitchen floor.

I open it and pull out a casserole pot, a skillet, and a couple of sauce pots. I notice a cookie sheet. He has plates and cups wrapped in newspaper.

"Don't tell my mom," he says.

"You're a pottery thief."

"She won't miss them."

He goes outside to his car and comes back with a bag of groceries. He reaches inside and retrieves a carton of eggs, a stick of butter, some apples, grapes, and a broccoli crown.

"You need folic acid," he says. Reaching in, he pulls out a jar of kosher pickle spears. "For late-night cravings."

I look inside and see a box of saltines.

"You still have morning sickness?" he asks.

"No. Your mom made a tea, and it really helped."

"She loves making remedies from back home."

"When was the last time you visited the Philippines?"

"I was in seventh grade, I think."

"How was it?"

"I remember it always raining, and the streets were congested."

"How were your relatives?"

"You want to know how they treated me?"

"Yes."

"It didn't matter to them that I was half Black," he says. "What's crazy is when I lived in Alabama, my color was all my relatives there talked about. Everybody said I was Grandmother's favorite because I looked different from my other cousins. She always talked about my 'good, curly hair' and my 'nice light skin.'"

"Do you wonder how our baby will look?"

"Yes."

He kneels so he is even with my stomach to kiss it. With the palm of his hand, he rubs my belly. "It'll be beautiful like you and handsome like me," he says. "Have you felt it kick yet?"

"It's still early."

He kisses my stomach. "Got to make sure we eat right."

Before long, he slices and washes strawberries and grapes, arranging them in a bowl. Next, he butters four slices of bread to toast in the oven. He waits until the bread is golden brown before taking it out. Next, he cracks four eggs into a bowl to whisk. Meanwhile, butter melts in a skillet on the stove. He sprinkles a little salt and pepper on the eggs before adding them to the skillet where he scrambles until the eggs are fluffy and ready. We eat them scrambled easy with fruit and dry toast.

"What ever happened to Lilly and Benny?" I ask, remembering hanging out with them in a couple of clubs this past summer. Lilly is an actress who co-stars in a highly rated television sitcom. She and JB dated once. Her boyfriend Benny is an up-and-coming rock musician.

"I don't see them much anymore. I think Lilly's back in New York taping the show. Benny's busy trying to get his career going. He's a Black man out here performing rock and roll."

"He's a novelty like me."

"Do you think that works in your favor?"

"Sometimes."

"Do you feel pressured?" he asks.

"It can be a bit overwhelming at times. I overcompensate by practicing and giving everything I have."

Moments later, I'm sitting at the piano practicing for my performance tonight, using a metronome to help me keep the tempo. Meanwhile, JB's cleaning up the kitchen. When he's finished, he sits next to me on the piano bench. I play Bach's "Concerto No. 1 in D Minor BWV 1052." I'm so focused on mastering my technique and timing that I ignore him. He watches quietly then applauds once I finish.

"Bravo. That's beautiful," he says.

"Are you coming to my performance?"

"I can't. I've got a scrimmage."

"That's too bad."

"I'm getting the best show right now. This is priceless, Maddie."

"Thank you."

I don't know why, but I'm starting to get nervous. I don't want

L.A. Phil to know about my pregnancy. I may seem a bit paranoid when I say this, but in rehearsals, during awkward pauses in conversations with some of the musicians, they look at me, and I read their expressions. They want to ask the question, and what if by chance they ask? Do I tell them? Or is it none of their business?

# Eleven

Days later, JB shows up with a letter in hand.

"What's that?" I ask.

"The results from the paternity test."

"Open it."

He quickly opens it, and together we read, and when we finish, we look at each other. The look in his eyes is relief and pure joy. We kiss and hold each other close. He rubs my stomach. We laugh, and it's a strange release, a chance to finally exhale. I always knew.

"We have to show this to your daddy."

"Get dressed," he tells me.

"Why? Where are we going?"

"I want to see the look on his face."

I wash up, brush my hair into a ponytail, and put on lip gloss with a feeling of gratification. I want to see the look on his face, too.

Once we arrive, Judy is in the kitchen, and the aroma smells like chicken with herbs and seasoning. She appears to be in a happy mood. She greets both of us with warm hugs and kisses. She gently rubs my stomach.

"How many weeks now?"

"Fourteen."

"Still nauseous?"

"No, though I would like more of the tea."

"It's good, right?" she asks before going to the oven and pulling out a tray of what looks like rolls.

"*Hopiang baboy,*" she says to us.

JB and I sit on island barstools, and like little children, we anticipate tasting it.

JB says something to Judy in a foreign language. With a spatula, she scoops up a roll from the pan and blows it to cool before taking a bite. She scoops up two more, placing them on napkins and setting them before us.

"What's the language? I didn't know you spoke it," I say to JB.

"It's Tagalog. I only know that much." He indicates a small amount with his fingers. "And a few curse words."

"This is delicious," I say. "How do you stay so tiny eating all this food?"

"I don't know. Genetics," she says, shrugging it off.

"I wish I could eat whatever I wanted and stay the same size."

"Where's Pops?" JB asks his mother.

"I'm right here." We hear his voice, and he appears, walking into the kitchen. He's calm as he pulls up a chair to sit next to us at the island. Right now, I feel nervous. To me, James has always been dry. I wonder how he and Judy have stayed married so long. They are so different. She is open and talkative. She doesn't really have to know you, and yet you come away knowing her life story. James, on the other hand, as Daddy would say, must "size you up" before determining whether he wants to deal with you. His stare is piercing. Like right now, he's quiet. I glance at JB, who's looking at his father, gauging his expression.

"I have something," JB says as he hands his father the letter.

"What's this?" James removes a pair of reading glasses attached to his shirt collar.

He sets the glasses on the bridge of his nose and proceeds to read. Judy stops what she's doing and joins him in reading the letter. Once he finishes, he takes off his glasses and looks up from the letter at us.

"So?" I hear JB ask.

Judy smiles and claps her hands. She gives us both a hug. We all stop to see James' reaction.

"*Ummm*—" James seems to measure his words carefully. "I read it. I see the results and *ummm...* You've got to hit the ground running."

I glance at JB, and he's lingering on every word.

"From the time you were seven, we worked on developing your skills to get you to the level you are now. Thirteen years is a long time to pour and invest in someone. One valuable lesson that this ordeal has taught me: What I want and what you want are entirely different. I want what any parent wants for their children: good health, tremendous wealth, and much success. You want to start a life with a girl you barely know."

"You used to tell me, no matter what challenges you face, know they happen so you can grow and be better," JB says.

"This is so unnecessary, son," James responds.

"Know what else you used to tell me? The greater the obstacle, the more glory in overcoming it," JB answers.

"Apparently you missed the part where I said don't be a fool, cover your tool. Plug your funnel before you enter the tunnel. Remember me saying that?"

JB is silent and in deep thought. "I'm ready to make that call," he says.

"Okay," James says.

"When?" Judy asks.

"Now," JB says. "Get the agent on the phone."

James grabs a phone. It's a cordless one where you raise the antennae. James dials the number and gives the phone to JB. After three rings, I hear a female's voice answer. JB makes small talk before he's put on hold. Judy wipes her hands on a towel and stands between James and me. I hear a man's voice pick up on the other end. JB makes more small talk and banter before he gets serious.

"It's time," he says, breathing a sigh of relief. "After spring semester, I'm declaring myself eligible for the draft."

I notice Judy give James a squeeze and a hug. When JB hangs up the phone, Judy gives him a warm hug. The expression on his face is relief. James turns to me.

"I hope you're ready for what's to come," he says.

I take a deep breath.

"This is a huge step. Now the eyes of the sports world will watch his every move," James adds.

I understand in a way. "How do you feel?" I ask JB.

"It hasn't hit me yet," he says.

"Oh, it will," James says.

\*\*\*

Our next stop is Aunt Mary and Uncle Frenchy's to get my mail and messages Gilda might've left because I still don't have a phone. I haven't visited in some time. Although I still have a key, I choose to knock, unsure of what to expect now that JB and I are together. Caleb opens the door. The look on his face when he sees us together reflects the disappointment he still feels inside.

"Hi, Caleb," I speak.

"Cuzzo." He invites us in. We hug. The interaction between him and JB still feels odd but obligatory. They make small talk. Caleb plops down on the sofa and brings the phone back to his ear.

"They're out by the pool," he says and resumes his conversation in a hushed tone.

Outside, Aunt Mary and Uncle Frenchy lounge. She sips wine. Whatever he's sipping is brown.

"Look who finally decides to drop in and check on us little

people," Uncle Frenchy says. It feels good hugging them. I sit next to Aunt Mary. JB sits in a chair across from us.

"How's it going in Santa Monica?" Aunt Mary asks.

"Great. Guess who we ran into?"

"Who?"

"Rosie."

"Rosie? In Santa Monica?"

"Yes. We saw her on the pier," I lie. I don't want to say she was working.

"You talked to her? How is she doing?" Aunt Mary asks.

"Great, and she looks good, too."

"I don't know why she hasn't stopped by to see me."

"Maybe she'll drop in when you least expect it," I say.

I glance at JB sitting comfortably in the lounge chair across from us.

"Got some good news," he says with a smile.

"We like good news," Uncle Frenchy responds.

"Got the results from the paternity test," JB says.

"If it's good news, I say congratulations." Aunt Mary turns to me. "You can finally lay James' doubts to rest. What did he say?"

"Not much," JB answers, "but I've got more good news."

Aunt Mary and Uncle Frenchy sit up in anticipation.

"I've declared myself eligible for the upcoming draft."

Aunt Mary and Uncle Frenchy are silent for a minute before reacting.

"Congratulations," Uncle Frenchy says. "I take it you haven't told Caleb yet."

"No."

"I'm excited for you but sad. All these years, you and Caleb played side by side. It's going to be different after this season not seeing you two together on the court."

JB nods. I like seeing this calm, gentle side of him.

"What is Caleb doing?" Aunt Mary asks.

"He's on the phone," I respond.

"You have what it takes," Uncle Frenchy says to JB. "Did Maddie's pregnancy prompt you to make this decision now?"

"Yes," he answers.

"You've got a lot coming at you," Uncle Frenchy says.

"Frenchy, you know me. I'm like a 747—I fly above it."

"You do that," Uncle Frenchy says.

"I'm cruising. The ride might get bumpy, but I'm not falling."

Seems JB's giving himself a pep talk. I imagine he does this right before a game.

"Keep that winning attitude," Aunt Mary says.

The four of us are silent. I hear birds chirping, a chopper flying, and police sirens in the distance.

"I know you don't approve of me and Maddie's relationship," JB begins. "You believe I'm not the right person for her."

"Both of you ought to be focusing on school, but instead you're making plans to have a baby," Uncle Frenchy says, "as if being young and a teenager is not already difficult enough."

"I'll be here for Maddie and the baby." I notice the sincerity in his eyes. "I love her."

"Love?" Uncle Frenchy sits back in his chair. "You just got out of diapers."

JB and I find his remark funny.

"I'm serious. Love comes with experience," he says. "Don't confuse it with infatuation."

"No, Frenchy, I've been infatuated," JB says. "This is different."

"You're young. Trust me, that feeling will pass." Uncle Frenchy waves him off.

"I know true love when I feel it," JB declares.

"Will you love her when you get lonely on your road trips and a groupie who looks like she came off the cover of *Playboy* knocks on your door at three in the morning?" Aunt Mary asks.

JB nods affirmatively. "Yes, I will."

"Will you still love her when she's exhausted and can't think straight, and she's screaming at you with milk dripping down her breasts, and she tells you no, she can't stroke your ego because you lost a championship game?"

This time JB just stares at Aunt Mary like she's crazy. He doesn't blink.

"*Love* at your age, and in your position is tested on the regular." She takes a sip from her glass of wine. "The odds of passing the test are stacked against you."

"Mary, why don't you do a study about them then write a book and title it *Young Love in the 1980s: Can It Survive Temptations?*" Uncle Frenchy chuckles.

"Aunt Mary, weren't you a teenager when you met Uncle Frenchy?" I ask.

"That was a different time, and I was nineteen when we met. I was twenty when we married. I was twenty-two when Caleb was born."

"You were just five years older than me," I say.

"That is true, but I was ten years ahead in wisdom and experience," she says.

"Already, everyone's throwing in the towel on us," JB says. "Give us a chance. I used to be a wolf. Now, I'm a lamb, thanks to Maddie," JB declares.

Aunt Mary and Uncle Frenchy burst into laughter, the kind where they are tipsy and leaning on each other.

"You kids are killing me," Uncle Frenchy says, wiping away a tear.

JB is contemplative sitting in the chair. I sense his frustration with everyone doubting us. *How can we fall in love so fast?*

We leave Aunt Mary and Uncle Frenchy laughing. Meanwhile,

inside, Caleb is now slouched on the couch, still talking on the phone. JB sits next to him. Whomever Caleb is talking to has him smiling. He glances at JB and covers the receiver.

"What?"

"Tell her you'll call her back," JB instructs him.

"I don't want to."

"This is really important what I'm about to tell you."

"Hey," Caleb says, "let me call you back." He hangs up. "Spill it."

"I'm telling you before I tell the rest of the team: I'm turning pro after next semester."

Caleb's reaction is the same as his parents'. "No freaking way."

"I've got to," JB says.

"Wow, man." Caleb sits up.

"It's the best move for me."

"Congratulations." Caleb offers his hand.

JB's facial expression is a combination of shock mixed with relief. He shakes Caleb's hand.

"Thanks, bro," JB says.

"Handle your business, I'll hold it down and fight on." Caleb nods.

"I appreciate that," JB responds as they do their secret handshake.

Tears blur my eyes. I get the sense that they are slowly getting back on track.

I grab my mail, and on the ride back to Santa Monica, JB and I stop at a baby boutique. Once inside, I see baby cribs with accessories, strollers, and clothing from newborn to the age of five. I pick up a baby clothing ensemble for a newborn baby girl that includes tiny crocheted pink-and-white shoes. JB picks up a stuffed toy and pulls the string. A lullaby plays in a soft bell tone. We hold hands and walk in silence, stopping when something catches our eye. I see a cream for stretch marks, and I grab it.

"I'll need you to rub this on my tummy."

He reads the label. "Grab another. You can never have too many."

And that's what he does when we get to my place. He rubs, talks, and sings to my belly before eventually falling asleep with one hand resting on my stomach.

# Twelve

*October 17, 1987 9:18 pm*

*When JB announced to the public his decision to turn pro, the tidal wave that followed engulfed us, sweeping us and tossing us in opposite directions. It's been two weeks, and I haven't talked to him. I happen to be visiting Aunt Mary and Cassandra when I see him on television. He's at a press conference with his coach on one side and his father on the other. He's being asked questions, but I'm not listening to what he's saying, I'm looking at his facial expressions the way his eyes dance when he's explaining something, the way his mouth moves, the colors of his uniform, and the way they blend perfectly with his skin tone, which is the color of desert sand. I'm mesmerized and can't take my eyes off the screen. I remember it's been days since we last communicated, then I get angry. To keep busy, I create music so I'll forget about him. Then there are times when I'll hear a song, and I am reminded of us. In my randomness of thoughts, I see our feet—my dainty foot against his size-fifteen foot and our legs entwined. Then the warmest of feelings consume me, and it's during this I'm kicking myself for getting caught up.*

\*\*\*

Sometimes the silence inside the townhouse speaks to the point of deafening. I open my backpack and pull out my compositions, seeing all the music I started writing from age twelve until now. The pages are faded. Some have turned yellow from the wear and tear. Gilda's already set up a publishing company for me. Now it's time to get this music out. I want to hear it rolling off the instruments in an orchestra or accompanying a dramatic scene in a movie or the backdrop of an opera. I might not have *Juilliard trained* behind my name just yet, but I will have a symphonic orchestra interpreting my work soon.

I get out of the townhouse and take a walk. The neighborhood is busy with people walking their dogs, joggers holding a steady pace, and people on a leisurely stroll. The breeze off the Pacific makes it windy. When I get to a bus stop shelter, I sit and wait. I don't have a car, so I've learned to navigate by riding the bus. First time was scary. I didn't know what to do or where to get off. I didn't know about transfers or ringing the bell to alert the driver of my stop. Some of the people who ride are scary looking. They stare at you with curious eyes. The bus arrives, I pay my fare, and find the nearest seat. I notice a guy sitting across from me wearing a pair of headsets bobbing his head, reminding me of JB. He has a portable Sony Walkman player. He stops bobbing to open the device to flip the tape to the other side before he resumes the bobbing. Looking out the window, I see throngs of people on the beach. The sunlight reflects off parts of the ocean, at times casting a blinding glare. It's crazy how my brain works, and music is constantly on it. I hear a C7, one of the highest octaves on the piano. I imagine myself striking the key while my foot holds and releases the sustain pedal. I get off at the next stop and cross the street to go inside the McDonald's lobby. I see Rosie working her spot at the drive-thru window. I order a Big Mac with fries and a Sprite from another worker at one of the registers. Rosie notices me and smiles but continues working for some time. I pace myself and eat slow, but I still finish before she takes a break.

"How long is your break?" I ask.

"I'm about to clock out. Hold on."

She disappears behind the counter. There is a slew of other workers, each one busy doing something. The place is a zoo. I got here just in time because the lines are much longer. Rosie reappears. She's taken off her work shirt and replaced it with another top. She's removed her work visor and let down her hair. It hangs to her shoulders. I'm thinking she wants to sit down and talk. She beckons me to follow her outside.

"How far do you live from here?" she asks.

"Not far, but I want to take the bus. It drops us off a couple of blocks from where I live," I say to her.

She glances at me, like she's trying to figure out something, but she remains quiet instead. We wait for a bus. "You like working here?" I ask.

"It's okay," she answers, sounding uncertain.

The bus arrives, and minutes later, it drops us off two blocks from the townhouse. I walk slow. Rosie notices.

"Are you okay? You seem kind of tired."

I don't want to tell her why because I still want her to look at me as a big sister who's got it together.

"I just ate a Big Mac."

"Sounds like you've got the 'itis,'" she says.

I notice she's carrying a different red backpack. It's a little bigger than the one she had this summer.

"What is 'itis'?" I ask.

"You haven't heard of the 'itis'? It's when you get tired after eating."

"Oh, then I guess I have it." I chuckle.

Once inside the townhouse, Rosie looks around and walks straight to the patio to look out.

"It's nice," she says.

"Are you still living with your boyfriend?" I ask.

"Yes."

"Don't you think you should go back home?"

"The state came and took my brothers and sisters because my momma started locking them up in the closet, claiming she was protecting them from stray bullets."          .

"Are your brothers and sisters together?" I ask.

"I don't know." Rosie's attitude is nonchalant. She opens her backpack and pulls out a McDonald's bag. She retrieves a burger wrapped in paper and an apple pie.

"I'll split it with you," she says.

"No thanks."

She bites and chews in a hurried rush. I've never known her to eat at such a rapid pace. Her burger is finished within minutes, and so is the apple pie.

"Are you in school?"

"Yes."

I notice the time. It's a little after seven o'clock in the evening. With the time change about to happen, the evenings are darker sooner.

"How late do you work?"

"Sometimes until closing."

"Then how do you get home?"

"I take the last bus. It runs at eleven. Sometimes I don't get home until after midnight."

"And you're not afraid?"

"Why do you always ask me that, Maddie? I can't be scared. I do what I gotta do."

"When it's late and you don't want to go home, you can always come here."

"Then how will I get to school? You don't have a car."

"I guess you'll get up extra early."

"I'm not trying to do that. I'm less than ten minutes away from school. If I spent the night here, it'll take me an hour with traffic." She smacks her lips. "What do you have to drink?"

"Look in the fridge."

She strolls to the refrigerator to open it. "Dang, Maddie."

"Sorry. I need to go grocery shopping."

Rosie searches the cabinets, finding a glass. She turns on the kitchen faucet and fills it with water. I can hear her gulping it, hurriedly followed up with a satisfactory breath of relief.

"I gotta go," she says. My heart races when I think of her walking to the bus stop alone in the dark.

"Let me call you a cab," I say, relieved I finally have a phone.

"And watch them freak out once I tell them where I want to get dropped off?"

"Why would they do that?"

"Maddie, I don't live in a nice neighborhood like this. I live in the hood. There are no cabs around here that will drive me to the J's."

"Then why did you choose to work at *this* McDonald's?"

"Because these people don't question my age. If I tell them I'm sixteen, they believe me. That's why I'm going to keep working here."

"I hope you stay in school."

"Maybe."

"Don't think about dropping out. Get your diploma. Your art is so good. You can get a job doing animation."

"I know."

"What have you sketched lately?"

She reaches inside her new backpack and pulls out her sketch-pad, flipping until she comes to a page. The image is an over-the-shoulder view of a guy standing behind two turntables.

"Your boyfriend, Dante?"

"Yes."

The sketch is detailed and descriptive. Dante is a deejay. She pays close attention to the detail of the buttons on the mixing machine and the placement of his fingers on the records.

"This is phenomenal, Rosie."

"Thank you."

"Promise me you'll stay in school," I hear myself say.

"Weren't you supposed to be going away to school?" Her question catches me off guard.

I still don't want her to know about the pregnancy. Unless I point it out, my pregnancy isn't so obvious.

"An opportunity I couldn't pass up happened," I tell her, referring to my limited obligation with L.A. Phil.

She doesn't ask me to explain, and I don't.

"I like your place. Now that I know where you live, I'll drop in."

"You have my number. Call me if you can."

She nods. Draping her backpack over one shoulder, she walks out the door. I watch her walk to the end of the sidewalk. Her gait is determined and quick. She waits at the corner of the street, taking one more glance at me before crossing the street and picking up her pace.

The following week when I go to the McDonald's, she isn't there. A week later, I go, and she isn't there. My heart sinks. I ask a coworker if he's seen the cute little black girl with the ponytail who always works the window. He tells me he hasn't seen her in two weeks. It was two weeks when I last saw her walk out my front door. My heart drops.

\*\*\*

Ursula picks me up. We've been invited to a Halloween party in West Hollywood. She's dressed as the Princess Bride. I'm wearing a pink empire-waist baby doll dress with black flat Mary Janes. My hair is parted down the middle with two shoulder-length ponytails and accented with hair ribbons.

"Let me guess: Dorothy from *The Wizard of Oz*," she says in a perky and excited way.

"No. A Cabbage Patch Kid."

Her expression changes. I notice a frown. "Oh."

"I couldn't think of anything else, and I don't want this to seem so obvious," I say pointing to my growing belly.

"Mona flew in from New York last night. She'll be at the party."

Mona is a friend of ours who moved to the East Coast, and now she's modeling and doing television shows based in New York City.

"Good. I can't wait to see her." I try to sound upbeat and cheerful, but Rosie is in the back of my mind. "Hey, can we stop by the McDonald's near Colorado and Ocean Avenue?"

"Sure. Are you craving fries?" she asks.

"I am." This time, I'm hoping Rosie's there, but when I place my order for fries and a Sprite, I hear another voice, and when we pull up to the drive-thru window to pay, there's no Rosie. The greasy, salty potato scent triggers my nausea, something I haven't experience in a while. I lose my appetite.

"Pull over, please," I tell Ursula.

"You okay?"

"No."

She whips the car over and comes to a stop. I open the door and erupt on the pavement. Blood rushes to my head, making me dizzy. I hold on to the door for support, waiting for this feeling of dreadfulness to pass.

*Rosie is okay. Maybe she stopped working to focus on school.*

I wipe my mouth and close the door, feeling as if I've been shaken violently and bashed into the pavement. I take a sip of Sprite, close my eyes, and rest my head against the seat. "I don't want to go home."

"You need to change. Your costume is hideous."

I look at my dress, and laughter that's buried, hidden under mounds of anxiety, comes out to the point where tears roll down my cheeks. Ursula looks at me like I'm losing it. Between the pregnancy, not hearing from JB, and now Rosie, I guess I am.

"What?" she asks.

"I can't do this."

"What's wrong?"

"I can't do this." I point to my belly.

She takes my hand. "Get a grip, okay? You can do anything." She takes a strand of wild hair and tucks it behind my ear.

I nod. Coming from Ursula, it's sincere.

"Every day is not going to be good, but you get through it," she says.

"Okay," I agree.

"Dry your tears. We're going to the party, and if anyone asks, tell them you're Carrie from the Stephen King novel."

We laugh as she lets down the top on her convertible BMW. The car accelerates, and the wind off the Pacific becomes a blast of drums in my ears. I scream. It's a release, and Ursula, being my friend, truly understands.

# Thirteen

I see Mona, tall, slim, dressed in an off-the-shoulder costume, and I am self-conscious. She's with her boyfriend, Ruger, who also happens to be my ex, Gregory's best friend. Mona and I greet, cheek-to-cheek, followed up with something that resembles a hug where we barely touch.

"A Cabbage Patch Kid," I say before she asks.

"Pebbles and Bamm-Bamm," she responds, pointing to herself and Ruger whose costume shows off his muscular physique. He excuses himself. He isn't one with many words to begin with, but part of me wonders if Gregory's told him about us. As Mona and I talk, she doesn't seem to act as though she knows. She's on an end-less loop about New York City, modeling, and acting. I'm glad in a way, so I won't have to talk about me.

While she talks, I scan the room noticing guests dressed in every-thing from Gumby to extravagant costumes with feather headpieces, boas, and rhinestones.

"I know New York City is huge, but I'd at least thought we'd bump into each other," Mona says to me.

"I'm still here in L.A.," I tell her.

"Oh? Do tell." She crosses her long, lean legs and angles herself forward.

"L.A. Phil liked my guest performance so much they invited me back as a guest pianist until the end of November."

"Congratulations."

"Juilliard's on hold for now."

"How are you and Gregory?" she asks.

Just as she asks, Gregory appears dressed as a pirate. I open my mouth to speak, but words and sounds run in the opposite direction.

"Maddie." Mona waves a hand in front of my face.

I snap out of my daze and into reality. I haven't seen Gregory since the day I told him I was pregnant. That day, he gave me a kiss—a long, lingering, intense kiss, the kind that makes your knees buckle. The kind of kiss that when you think about it, it still gives you butterflies.

*Why is this happening?*

Mona's talking, but her voice sounds like an endless loop of noise. Gregory's laughing with other guests. His mouth is opened so wide I can see his teeth, and in the dimly lit room, I can't help but notice their whiteness. As he gets closer, I can almost smell him—the fresh, light, and airy scent of his cologne. Gone are the horn-rimmed glasses that used to make him look dorky. He sports a pirate's hat and a patch over one eye. He walks around like he owns the place.

*If he comes over, what do I say—or do I say anything?*

Mona finally stops talking and walks up and grabs his hand. At that moment, Gregory and I lock eyes, and I notice him squint as if his eyes are playing tricks. He removes the patch from the other eye to get a better look. He freezes.

I don't know what to do with myself at this point. I'm sitting as I was taught as a little girl in etiquette class with my legs crossed at the ankles. He's not sure what to do with himself. I see a painful expression in his eyes.

"You guys, stop acting like strangers." Mona's head moves as if she's watching a tennis match.

Gregory looks like he wants to cry. My heart feels like it's about to leap out my mouth.

"Guys," Mona says as she's finally become aware of the tension.

"I'm out." He turns and walks away.

"Gregory." She follows him, talking until he waves her off. She returns, perplexed.

"What's happening?" she asks.

I shrug it off, feeling tears blur my eyes.

"Is it really bad?" she asks.

"I don't want to talk about it."

She sits next to me. "You've broken up?"

Clearly, she isn't listening when I tell her I don't want to talk. "I'll tell you another time," I say to her.

"Fine." She stands and walks to another part of the house.

Now I feel lost in this crowd, hidden behind costumes and dim lights. The music is loud, but not so loud that I can't hear the person next to me. Just like all parties, I feel like an outsider—that I don't belong and the only reason I'm around people is because I don't want to be sitting home alone with music being my only comfort. I walk outside on a terrace, and the October chill still isn't a deterrent for me. I stare out into the glimmer of L.A.'s twinkling lights. Even with this life growing inside me, I've never felt so alone.

*Why isn't JB talking to me? Why do I have this feeling that Gregory and I have unfinished business?*

I don't want to go down that road again. Gregory and I had fun, but with him, there seemed to be something missing. I hear my teeth chattering, and I glance and see a couple—he's dressed as Peter Pan; she's dressed as Snow White—locked in an embrace, kissing.

"Maddie," Ursula calls.

"Hey."

"I saw Gregory," she says.

"I did, too."

"You guys talked?"

"No. He saw me and left."

"You mean he left the party?"

"He said, 'I'm out.' What does that sound like to you?"

"He left."

"I keep seeing the look on his face when I told him. He gave me that look tonight."

She glances at me, holding myself and shivering. "Let's go."

Inside, the party continues with couples dancing, people mingling, Mona and another girl who looks just like her dressed in a skimpy black leather cat suit are posing for a picture. Mona notices us and beckons us to get into the picture. I'm not feeling it, but I put on my best face and pose.

"Maddie, you've met my sister, Anna."

"No."

We exchange pleasantries, and my thoughts go back to a conversation I had with Cassandra about JB recently being involved with Mona's sister. She's gorgeous. Just like JB's ex-girlfriend Basha was gorgeous—gorgeous, like most people tell me I am.

As the evening progresses, I notice more people leaving and drifting into other rooms in the house. I lose Ursula, and I can only imagine what she's doing and with whom. In another room, people gather, conversing. On a large projector screen is a basketball game between USC and UCLA. I overhear someone saying it's just a scrimmage. My heart flutters when I see JB on television. It's like I'm looking at a different person. I only know it's him when the camera shows him up close. I notice his hair is shaved. He dribbles the ball effortlessly between his legs, handling it with his left hand just as well as the right. He's aggressive on defense, guarding his opponent, studying his move, almost knowing what he'll do next because he steals the ball, dribbling with the opponent hot on his trail and an opposing player soaring to his right aiming to block his shot, but JB reverses and uses his left hand to dunk it. The crowd goes wild. The move is executed so gracefully they show it once more in slow motion on instant replay.

On another play, Caleb has two opponents guarding him, but he spots JB running unguarded toward the basket. He passes him the ball, and JB scores with a layup. He points to Caleb and nods. I sit on the sofa and watch the game, wondering, *When will we see each other?*

*** 

I can't get Rosie off my mind. I call Aunt Mary. I don't mention Rosie working at McDonald's. I tell her that Rosie never called me like she promised, and now I'm worried. Aunt Mary says she'll call me back after she investigates. I pray nothing terrible has happened.

I take a break from practicing to spend time at the beach. The roar of the tide is calm and soothing so much at times I find myself nodding off, only to be awakened by the heaviness of my own head. I bring my backpack in case I get inspired, but something tells me to relax and be in the moment. My belly flutters. The sensation is strange yet miraculously beautiful. I wonder if I can be a good mother like my mother was or like Aunt Mary is. Daddy says the baby can sense my feelings, and if that's the case, I want this baby to know that sometimes I don't feel capable. I'm not ready. I don't care how much my conscious tells me I am. I don't want the baby to sense the selfishness I feel and how sometimes I care more about my relationship with JB than I do about making sure the baby hears the piano.

*** 

I am now in my twentieth week, the time when you find out the sex of the baby. Just when the nurse Rachael is about to put the gel on my stomach, I stop her.

"I don't want to know," I tell her.

Dr. Blue is nearby. "It's certainly your choice if you don't want to know," she says in an upbeat, cheerful tone. "Just let us check the baby's vitals and measurements, and you'll be on your way."

Aunt Mary sits across from me. "Now you'll have us all wondering," she says.

"I want it to be a surprise," I tell Aunt Mary.

"Right now, your baby should be responsive to sounds," Dr. Blue explains.

"I feel kicks and flutters whenever I play the piano," I tell her.

"Music stimulates the senses and promotes brain development," Dr. Blue says. "Music also provides the basis for a baby to pick up sounds and languages when they are born."

"I play classical, so I'm hoping the baby remembers."

"They can remember frequently played music up to year after they are born."

I touch my belly. It's growing, and I've gained more weight. Just like I don't want to know the sex, I don't want to know my weight. Afterward, Aunt Mary and I go to her favorite Italian restaurant where she orders a glass of cabernet and a bowl of mussels. I order minced veal with rigatoni.

"You plan to have a baby shower?" she asks.

"I haven't given it much thought."

"I see." She sips and thinks about something. "Would you like a shower?"

"I think I would, though I want it to be very low key—maybe ten guests."

"Why don't we have it at my home."

"That would be great," I say aloud, but my thoughts are elsewhere, thinking, *How much longer can I appear as if I'm not pregnant?* Yesterday, I purchased my first maternity top. Not the most flattering, but then again maternity wear isn't designed to flatter. I also purchased a dress. When I tried it on and turned sideways to see my profile, I wanted to cry. This is so mind-blowing. Sometimes it's hard to process.

I've been in the townhouse for some time, and today is the first time Aunt Mary comes inside. She surveys the room we're in. I only have the piano as furniture.

"It's nice. How are you liking your independence?" she asks.

"It was fun not having responsibilities," I admit.

"The adult life. Not all it's chalked up to be, huh?"

"It has its fun moments," I say.

She walks through the dining area to the patio door. I have the blinds open. She pulls them back to look outside. "Have you met your neighbors?" she asks.

"No."

She turns and walks to the spiral staircase leading up to the loft. "What's upstairs?"

"Nothing."

"Who told you about this place?" she asks.

"JB."

"I see." She looks around as if she's seen little to enough. "When you get tired of paying an arm and a leg for rent, our door is always open."

I thank her and walk with her outside to her car.

"You're not too far from the beach. You can walk there. It's good for you and the baby. Helps with a quicker delivery." She places a hand on my stomach. "I say you're having a girl," she says before opening the car door and sitting inside.

I get a little excited. "How can you tell?"

"I just know these things."

I feel sad when she drives away.

I return inside to play a little on the piano before I take out my journal and start writing.

*November 12, 1987, I guess it's three o'clock in the afternoon. Also Thursday.*

*Time flies. I have two more weeks left in my obligation with L.A. Phil. My last performance is the Wednesday before Thanksgiving, and so far, I've made it without anyone noticing. It doesn't hinder my playing, and I'm sure my ability to deliver is all that matters. At the concert-performance level, I'm of a limited group of Black people. I want to give the impression that all my time is devoted to music. I run the risk of not getting invited to perform with premiere symphonic orchestras if I project an image that is less than wholesome. This is not written, but implied.*

I decide to check the mailbox. Upon opening it, I see a letter in a six-by-nine bubble mailer from JB. *Wow. Too busy to pick up the phone?* I open the letter to see a cassette tape with the words: *JB's Soundtrack for Maddie.* Each song is numbered beginning with Side A: 1. *I Need Love* by LL Cool J 2. *I Just Can't Stop Loving You* by Michael Jackson 3. *You Are My Lady* by Freddie Jackson 4. *Tender Love* by Force M.D.'s 5. *Lady in my Life* by Michael Jackson 6. *Hello* by Lionel Richie 7. *Make Me Say It Again Girl* by The Isley Brothers.

Side B is all Prince songs 1. *Adore* 2. *Slow Love* 3. *Venus de Milo* 4. *Take Me with You* 5. *Do Me Baby.* 6. *The Beautiful Ones*

I open the letter. It reads:

*Monday, November 9, 1987*

*Maddie,*

*This is what crazy looks like. I've called you more than once, but I see your life is as crazy as mine. Our first game is in North Carolina the day after Thanksgiving. Believe me, I want to be around to go with you to the doctor visits. I still regret I couldn't make it for the first one. Send me pictures. I miss you. I got so much I want to write, but it's late. I hope you like the music. When you listen, I want you to think about us. Maybe one day during the break we can listen to it together. Until then.*

I wish I had a tape player. More than that, I wish he were here to sing to me. I'm counting down the days.

# Fourteen

"Ladies and gentlemen, presenting, debutante Cassandra Mary Kay Honoré."

Cassandra appears center stage dressed in a flowing white ball gown with white gloves. Uncle Frenchy, dressed in a tuxedo, stands tall and proud to her right. Aunt Mary, glowing in a golden designer gown, stands to her left. Kyle stands next to Aunt Mary, dapper in a black tuxedo. Aunt Mary presents a round bouquet to Cassandra before they embrace, then Cassandra comes forward, and as a drumroll sounds, she curtsies with a slight bow of her head. The curls of her sandy hair fall forward cascading like a waterfall. Applause rings, especially from our table. She graciously extends her hand to Uncle Frenchy who assists her to her feet before escorting her around the ballroom floor.

"Debutante Honoré is the daughter of Frances and Dr. Mary May Honoré. She is a senior at Westlake Preparatory Academy, a member of the student council, Jack and Jill of America, Inc., the Black Leadership and Culture Club, the Ethics Bowl, and varsity tennis. Upon graduation, she plans to attend the University of Southern California, eventually attending aviation school, and follow in her father's footsteps of becoming a commercial pilot."

"Impressive." Daddy turns to me. He and Gilda flew in as

Cassandra's guests. Last year, at my debutante ball in Houston, he was my escort, and we strolled proud under the ballroom lights as the mistress of the evening read off my credentials. I sounded promising. I remember the other mothers coming up to congratulate me and telling my father how proud they were of my accomplishments.

When he saw me today, I can tell my growing belly troubled him. He choked up and stammered, something I've never seen him do.

Sitting at Cassandra's guest table next to him and Gilda, I feel very much like I've let them down, that all I've worked for—hours I spent training, all the recitals, the concerti, the albums—were all for nothing. Who knows once I have the baby if I'll even have the motivation to keep playing. Life is just so uncertain. When Cassandra asked me to be a guest, I was reluctant. I wasn't sure if I could take being in the atmosphere and not feel a twinge of envy, listening to the mistress of ceremonies read off each girl's accomplishments, I want to tell each one to stay focused.

As I talk to Aunt Teal who's radiant in a plum-colored chiffon dress, I notice she's let down her hair and colored it, making her look years younger and refreshing. I am distracted when I hear the mistress of ceremonies say, "...escort is her cousin, Gregory Washington III." I see Gregory on stage standing next to the mother of the debutante he's escorting. He is broad shouldered; a hint of a smile traces his lips.

The mistress of ceremonies reads off his accolades: yachting enthusiast, freshman at Stanford.

*Freshman at Stanford? I'll have to ask Mona or Ursula about that.*

The evening progresses to Cassandra and Uncle Frenchy engaging in the father and daughter waltz. It's a regal display as the ladies are dressed in white. I learn Cassandra's gown is a Max V design. After the fathers do their dance, the debutantes are handed off to the escorts in a choreographed exchange. Cassandra and Kyle waltz along with Gregory and his debutante. The debutantes do a choreographed number with white parasols. Photographers capture the image on their cameras. I am in awe of Cassandra's beauty and graceful movements. When Uncle Frenchy and Aunt Mary join us at the table, they are so proud. I can see it in their expressions.

A nine-piece band plays live music for the party that follows. And just when I thought I could get through the night without having to face Gregory, we come face to face.

He scoffs, "Wow."

I notice his eyes do a quick study of my dress. It's a burgundy empire waist with lots of tulle. Ursula helped me pick it out. She even loaned me a diamond band to place on my ring finger. It caught Daddy and Gilda's eye earlier. So far, they haven't asked about it. Seeing Gregory, I get goose bumps. It's a tense and anxious feeling.

"Can we talk?" I ask.

"Talk? You've already shown how you felt."

"Can you at least let me explain, from the beginning?"

He looks at me, not sure whether he wants to hear what I have to say. He glances at a family gathered to take pictures. "Why don't we go to my suite upstairs and talk?"

"I'm not sure about that."

"Why? You afraid of me?"

"Now that you've mentioned it..."

"You're afraid of me? Now, that's the funniest thing I've heard yet." He chuckles. "You think I would hurt you?"

"I don't know."

"I could never hurt you the way you hurt me."

I tear up. "It wasn't intentional."

His eyes brim with tears. "I still can't believe what you did."

"When you left for Europe and I didn't hear from you, I thought that was it."

"You couldn't wait for me?" he asks.

"I was willing, however long it took. I was...I didn't think I was going to meet anyone else."

"You have no idea how it feels to want someone so bad. I never wanted anyone as much as I wanted you, Maddie, and you do this. You ripped out my heart from my chest, and while it was still beating, you held it up and squeezed it until it stopped."

I get a visual, and it's painful to see how callous I could be to someone whom I considered a friend. "I've got to go. I'm so sorry it didn't work out with us."

"My aunty Collette was about to throw you a party to celebrate your article in the magazine. I told her to axe it, and then I told her why."

Fresh tears roll down my cheeks. "It doesn't have to be this way."

"Oh, but it is. When I returned from Europe and we spent the day on my boat, you acted as though it was all new to you. Now I realize, it was just that—an act. You were taking your little secret to the grave—until you couldn't."

He notices the bracelet he gifted me gone from my wrist. "I see you took it off."

"I'm giving it back."

"Don't bother." His eyes brim with tears that refuse to fall.

We stand, both quiet.

"I hope you're happy," he says.

Without saying another word, he brushes past me and inside to the ballroom. I find a spot to sit because my legs are throbbing. I pull up my dress and notice my ankles are swollen. I find the nearest restroom and lock the door behind me. Luckily, there's no one inside but me, and no amount of tissue can stop the avalanche of tears that follows.

*** 

The following day, Aunt Mary calls to tell me she's located Rosie. She's in the last place she wanted to be: the foster care system.

"What's going to happen to her?"

"She's either placed in a group home or in a home with a foster parent."

"I hope they find her a nice home."

"When they become of age like Rosie, most people would rather not deal with them."

As I'm talking to Aunt Mary, I hear a knock at the door.

"We'll talk later," I tell her.

I peek through the keyhole, and to my surprise, I see my daddy and Gilda. In my haste to get ready for the debutante ball, I neglected to clean the place. I admit, cleaning up is not my specialty. It ranks right up there with cooking. I grab a can of Lysol to give the place a clean and refreshing scent before I finally open the door.

"Wow, I didn't think you were coming," I say to them.

They enter and look around. I still haven't furnished the place.

"I see you had no problem finding it, based on the address I gave you."

"We caught a cab," Daddy says, walking to the patio.

"It's my sanctuary for now." I'm feeling giddy and nervous.

Gilda approaches the piano and gathers my sheets of music. "So busy creating you forget to organize, right?" she asks, stacking them neatly with care and consideration.

"I want to put together an orchestra so I can hear how this sounds," I say to her.

Daddy looks around the place. "Who did you get to sign the lease for you?"

"My best friend, Ursula."

"How long is the lease?"

"It's month-to-month."

"How much is rent?"

"Twelve hundred."

He walks to the door of my bedroom. "May I?" he asks.

"Let me check something," I say.

I do a sweep of my room and bathroom to make sure I don't have anything on the floor like my bra and underwear. For the longest, JB's gym shorts and jockstrap lay on my bathroom floor.

"It's okay now, Daddy."

He walks inside and notices my unmade bed. I have clothing strewn across it. I can only imagine what he and Gilda are think-ing—*this place is chaos*, much like my life right now.

"This'll be a nice place once you tidy it up. Which brings me to this...it's time to come home," Daddy says once he's finished check-ing out the rooms. "Come home and get your life together. You and Gilda can plan what you need as far as the baby and your career."

"I don't want to."

"You don't have a choice." He stands firm.

I glance at Gilda for her to say something.

*Come to my rescue. Don't make me do this.*

"But I love it here. I have the sun, I have the beach, I have JB. You take all of it away from me, and I promise I'll die."

"I won't let you die, but I can't bear seeing you live in chaos and disarray."

"I can hire someone to clean and organize this place. Please, don't make me go home."

"Maddie, I'm up late every night praying and meditating, asking God to guide my steps, and His words keep repeating over and over: *Children, obey your parents in the Lord, for this is right.* You have no idea the guilt I feel for all these years putting the needs of my parishioners before you—assuming you will always do right because you're my daughter."

I feel a flutter, and naturally I hold my belly when that happens. Daddy notices, and I see that hurt and pain in his expression.

"Please, let me stay," I plead.

Daddy shakes his head. He's not budging. "We'll be in town until your performance this Wednesday, then we're leaving on the red-eye. I expect all your things packed. We'll figure out what to do with this." He pats the lid of my piano.

"I'll call a cab," Gilda says, picking up a Pacific Bell Yellow Pages.

"You just got here. Now you're leaving?" I ask, feeling the flutters happening again.

"Pack your bags, too. You're coming with us to the hotel to stay. You don't keep this place clean enough." Daddy says to me.

"But I can hire someone." I feel myself getting frustrated. "That's all I need to do. Other than that, there's nothing wrong."

"And that is what bothers me. You don't think anything's wrong," he says.

"I can't believe this." I'm crying as I go to my room to search for things to pack.

The thought of going back to Houston right now gives me so much anxiety I feel weak and lightheaded, but I manage to pack enough to take to the hotel. Once we're there, I crash on the sofa. Gilda places a pillow and a blanket out for me and orders fresh fruit and a bowl of chicken soup from room service. The sofa is where I remain, getting up twice to use the restroom. I don't touch the food. I don't have the desire to. I watch the glare of the outside light against the walls until the daylight fades into the evening. I go in and out of sleep, hearing Daddy and Gilda talking in hushed tones. I think they leave me alone at one point.

The next morning, I don't move, lying with the blanket over my head. I feel movement in my stomach, and these feel more like actual kicks. I think I have an appointment with Dr. Blue; I'm not sure. And that's another thing: If I go back to Houston, that'll mean getting a new obstetrician, and I really like Dr. Blue and her nurse, Rachael, and the rest of the staff at the office.

"Maddie," I hear Gilda's voice.

"Yes," I answer, still covered up to my head.

"You've got to eat something."

"I'm not hungry."

"But you have to eat."

She removes the blanket, and I must look a mess to her with my swollen red eyes, my red nose, and rosy cheeks. She rubs a hand over my forehead before offering me a glass of water.

"You remember you have a doctor's appointment today at eleven."

"What time is it?" I ask.

"A quarter after eight."

"Who's taking me, you or Aunt Mary?"

"I will."

"Why is he making me go back?"

"It's a struggle for your daddy to accept your situation."

"What difference does it make? If I were at Juilliard, I'd be in a similar situation living near campus in a small dormitory, probably half the size of my townhouse."

"With your daddy it's all about his convictions—what he feels is acceptable in God's sight. It keeps him awake at night, wrestling with the reality of seeing you pregnant, no husband to care for you, and no house with a white picket fence to raise your child—his first grandchild, Evelyn's first grandchild."

"But my townhouse is temporary. JB promised to get us a bigger place."

"That's not guaranteed, honey."

"But he found this townhouse. Plus, he really wants to do the right thing."

"Has JB's father come around now that he knows?"

"He's a little complicated."

"And the mother?"

"I really like her a lot. She wants to teach me how to cook."

Gilda reaches over to put some fruit and a croissant on a plate to give me. I nibble on a strawberry before eventually giving it back to her.

"Maddie, you have to eat, baby."

"I'm just not that hungry," I say before lying back on the sofa.

Later, Aunt Mary meets us at Dr. Blue's office. Dr. Blue and Gilda meet for the first time and exchange pleasantries and banter about their sororities.

We hear the fetal heart rate at 140 beats per minute. We gather to see the sonogram of the fetus. I watch Gilda's reaction. She smiles.

"Imagine an ear of corn. That's where you are at this stage."

Dr. Blue places a hand on my belly.

"You have any questions for me, Maddie?"

"No," I respond.

"You're so easy and laid back. I wish all my patients were like you." She smiles and turns to Gilda. "Pleasure to meet you." They engage in more banter before Dr. Blue is off to the next patient.

"I like her," Gilda says to Aunt Mary.

"Me, too," I say. The thought of leaving L.A. to go back home to Houston gets me emotional.

"What is it, Maddie?" Aunt Mary asks.

"Nothing." I suck up my tears.

"There's something. What's going on?"

Gilda talks, "Eugene wants her back in Houston."

Aunt Mary looks at me. "And you don't want to go."

"I'm fine out here. If I go back to Houston, it won't be good for me," I tell them.

"Eugene's not hearing it," Gilda says to Aunt Mary.

"She was fine living with us. Frenchy and I had no problem with that, but she insisted on moving out on her own, which I was never in favor of."

"I needed my own space where I can play my music any time I want. Since I've been in this townhouse, I've written over fifty songs.

You know how many songs I wrote this entire summer? Ten. The setting wasn't conducive to my creativity. You don't understand, I've got to be here. It's the only way I can stay sane."

"You know, Maddie, it's a bit of a challenge to assist you from fifteen hundred miles away," Gilda says.

"You would've had to do it if I went to Juilliard."

"I don't think I could effectively manage you from that distance," she says, and from the tone of her voice, she sounds tired.

Aunt Mary gives us a ride back to the hotel and joins us for dinner. I listen to them, and pick at my food. I'm still not having the best appetite. It's the week of Thanksgiving. The air is filled with scents of apple and cinnamon, sage, and pumpkin spice.

"We're flying back on the red-eye Wednesday night because Eugene is having Thanksgiving Day service at ten o'clock."

"Why Thanksgiving Day? That's time set aside for family?"

Gilda throws up her hands. "I stopped asking a long time ago." She chuckles.

Hours later, back at the hotel, after washing my face and brushing and flossing my teeth, I crash on the sofa. A knock on the door startles me. I get up slowly to answer, and it's Daddy from across the hallway.

"We need to talk," he says.

"I find my spot on the sofa. He sits on the opposite end. He's dressed casually, wearing a buttoned-up shirt and slacks.

"I keep you lifted in prayer constantly. There's a tug-of-war going on, and it's a battle between the spirit and the flesh. I want you to do the right thing and come home, but if coming home means watching you decline into depression, I don't want that."

"You're saying I can stay?"

He closes his eyes and slowly nods. The gray in his beard is becoming more visible and so are the worry lines on his forehead. Gilda enters the room and sits on the coffee table in front of us.

"Your father and I had a heart to heart, and this is what we've decided. No longer will I perform dual responsibilities of overseeing your career while being his assistant. I will work with you and you only. I will relocate here and stay for six months."

As she's telling me this, a warm sensation comes over me. I reach out and hug them both tight, promising myself that I will make them proud.

# Fifteen

My obligations with L.A. Phil are fulfilled. We perform before a full house, and judging from the roar and intensity of the applause in the end, I say we are spectacular. A reception follows, and after my meet and greet with patrons, this time with Gilda by my side, I bid thank yous to the company. I'm still thanking Gilda for making the sacrifice to move out here. Every day we brainstorm. I bounce ideas off her, and she gives me her opinion. Sometimes she just stares at me like I've lost my mind.

She's always reading newspapers and the trade magazines. Articles she reads she shares them with me. I'm sitting at the piano playing one of my songs, and she places a newspaper article in front of me. I stop when I notice a photo of JB wearing his school's jersey. The headline above it reads: *Star Player and Possible Top Draft Pick Impregnates Teen.*

The article doesn't mention my name; however, it mentions my age, and that I'm a piano prodigy—it even mentions me being the daughter of a prominent minister, displaying Daddy's name and that of the church. It's been a while since I had nausea, but after reading this article, a sick, bottomless feeling emerges. The writer's byline is underneath. I want to call the newspaper and ask to speak to this person, but Gilda is already on it.

"How does this happen, Gilda?" I ask once she gets off the phone.

"Any number of ways. Anything salacious or scandalous is open season for a hungry and desperate reporter."

I don't have a television set, but I get a call from Cassandra.

"Maddie, they're showing a report on JB and you."

"What are they saying?"

"That JB impregnated an underage girl and there's a possibility the state could look at a statutory rape charge."

"Statutory rape? They're making him sound like a creep." I hear my heart pounding.

"Lies," Cassandra's yelling at the television.

"What did they say?" I ask.

She doesn't answer right away. My guess she's trying to listen to the reporter. I can hear her television babbling in the background. "They're bringing Uncle Eugene into this. Unbelievable."

"I've got to go."

"Listen, I'm coming over to see you. Is it okay if I invite Ursula and Mona?" she asks.

"Sure," I say before hanging up.

I hear Gilda upstairs in the loft fussing with someone on the phone. I take a deep breath and count to ten, feeling the baby kick against the walls of my belly.

I realize today is the fifth anniversary of my mother's death, and this will be my first time not visiting her grave and putting a vase of fresh flowers on it. I find a spot in my living area to sit now that my townhouse is furnished and decorated. Gilda ordered furniture on Black Friday and had it delivered Saturday.

When she ends her conversation on the phone, she calmly walks downstairs and sits on the sofa next to me.

"If you are out and a reporter approaches you, don't say a word" is her advice to me.

"Will this hurt JB's chances of going pro?"

"I don't know, Maddie."

"And now Daddy's name and church are out there."

"The only good thing is that after forty-eight hours, people forget about a scandal—until the next big scandal comes along."

"But what's scandalous about this?"

"It's who it involves. I don't really follow sports, but from what I gather, your friend is a basketball phenom, and when you reach his status, you're put on a pedestal. You're also under a great deal of scrutiny. The same can be said for your daddy."

I hold on to my tummy, rubbing it, feeling the kicks, watching it stretch, thinking of the ocean of tears I've cried since discovering I was eight weeks pregnant on August 18.

Gilda calls Daddy, and he answers immediately. His voice is loud and distinct.

He answers the phone saying, "Yes, I know."

"What's happening there?" Gilda asks.

"This morning, reporters were camped out on the street badgering my parishioners." I hear him laughing. "My people didn't say a word."

"Good."

"How's Maddie?"

Gilda glances at me. "She's holding it together."

"I want to speak to her," he says.

Gilda hands me the phone. "Hello, Daddy."

"Hello, my love. I want you to know that I'm always talking to God about you. One minute I'm bragging on you, the next minute I'm talking bad about you." He chuckles. It's light-hearted and sweet. "But God always has a word for me, and He told me to tell you: 'My grace is sufficient.'"

"Yes, Daddy."

"We make mistakes, and our names get dragged through the

mud. Just know our sins got washed away on the cross, and because of that, we get His mercies, and we get His grace."

"Amen," I reply.

"You know what today is?"

"I do."

"I woke up early and picked some roses out of the garden that she planted when we first moved here."

"Mother loved her rose garden."

"Yes, indeed. I drove to the cemetery around six-thirty this morning, just before sunrise. I put the roses in a vase and set them at her grave—I didn't cry this time." He speaks in a slow, measured tone.

"That's good—I think." As I speak, I'm fighting back tears.

"She's with our Lord and Savior. That gives me comfort, and instead of crying, I rejoice."

"I love you."

"I love you, too. Before I go, if you hear from JB, please give him my personal number and have him call me right away."

"I will." I give the phone back to Gilda. They talk about the new assistant who's working for him. It's a guy this time. He's been around the ministry for as long as Gilda has, and if he's working for Daddy, it's someone he has a great deal of trust for.

Once she gets off the phone, she gathers her purse and her briefcase.

"If you need me, I'll be at the hotel for the rest of the evening."

"Will you find a place eventually?"

"Don't know, Maddie."

"May I ask, is everything okay with you and Daddy? I mean, I really appreciate you taking this huge step and coming out here, but if you and Daddy are in a relationship, isn't the distance a bit much?"

"It's a sacrifice I'm willing to make to see your dreams fulfilled."

I nod. I've got a village of people who believe in me, even at times when I doubt my own abilities. I walk with her outside to her car.

"I love you, Gilda."

She blows me a kiss before putting the car in reverse and driving off. An hour later, Cassandra, Mona, and Ursula arrive with shopping bags and a box of pizza. Seeing Mona's expression when I open the door is that of pure, genuine shock. By now, I thought she would've seen the reports on television or read the newspapers.

"May I?" she asks, reaching out to rub my stomach. "Oh my." Her voice is high pitched and dramatic.

I glance at Ursula and Cassandra who rolls her eyes.

"You act like you've never seen a pregnant woman before, Mona." Cassandra enters, carrying the box of pizza.

"Not one I know personally," Mona responds.

Ursula's holding three large shopping bags from a high-end store. Once inside, Mona and Cassandra look around the place. It's the first time for them both.

"I like it," Cassandra says.

"Me, too," Mona agrees.

"JB found it for us," I say, rubbing my belly.

"Have you talked to him?" Ursula asks.

"No."

"What do you think is going to happen?" Cassandra asks.

I shake my head, and they notice my sadness. Together they surround and embrace me in one big group hug.

"Where is he now?" Ursula asks.

"According to the basketball schedule, he's in Boston. Last night he was in North Carolina. Monday he'll be in Virginia. We haven't talked since he started getting ready for the season."

"When do you think you'll see him?" Mona asks.

"I don't know."

"I had no idea you two were a thing," Mona says. "Here I was talking to Gregory at the Halloween party. He said you broke up, but he never told me why."

"We stopped talking the day after I discovered." A hard kick interrupts my thoughts. "You guys see that?"

"See what?" Cassandra bites into a slice of pizza.

"It kicked."

"Do you know what you're having?" Mona asks.

"I want to be surprised."

"We got some things for the house," Ursula says, reaching inside one of the bags. She pulls out a box. "I got an answering machine for your phone. You record a greeting, and when you're not home, it'll take messages for you. Fancy much?" She winks, proud of her purchase.

"Thank you, Ursula."

"I got something, too," Cassandra says. "My gift is in the middle."

I reach inside a second bag and pull out a box containing monogramed bath sheets and hand towels and underneath that, a box containing monogramed plates and cups.

"I love it. Thank you," I say to Cassandra.

"Where's your TV?" she asks. "Maybe I should've given you that instead."

"It's coming," I tell her.

Mona has a shopping bag as well. I look inside and find a crystal figurine of a grand piano complete with the piano stool and a couple of crystal picture frames.

"Beautiful," I say to her. "Thank you."

"Are you having a baby shower?" Ursula asks.

"I am."

"I want to help," Ursula says.

"Me, too," Cassandra adds.

"Don't leave me out. I want to help, too," Mona says.

"We'll get it together soon," I say to them. "Can you bring me a couple of slices on my new monogramed plates, please?" I ask Cassandra before Mona and I sit on my sofa, and I place my feet across Mona's lap.

"Your hair and skin look amazing," she says to me.

"It's the prenatal vitamins."

"I heard prenatal vitamins are good for your skin and hair. What brand? Maybe I can get some," Mona says.

"You can't take them unless you're pregnant or trying to become pregnant."

"I can't?"

"No."

Cassandra hands me a plate with two slices of pizza.

"You have strange cravings?" Mona asks.

I bite into my slice and finish chewing before I answer. "Yes. I really like the Filet-O-Fish from McDonald's."

Mona makes a face. "McDonald's? You eat at McDonald's?"

"I like the fries, too," I add.

"The fries are good," Ursula says, "especially when they're hot and loaded with salt."

Mona waves a dismissive hand. I notice she's lost more weight now that she's modeling in New York City. Her face is skinnier, and her cheekbones are more pronounced. The top she's wearing fits snug around her enhanced breasts. With her father being a plastic surgeon, she gets a lot of unnecessary work done. The same could be said for her sister, Anna.

"Anna is gorgeous."

"Thank you. You know my sister is a publicist."

"I had no idea."

"She works with JB as well."

"She does?"

"You didn't know?"

"No." I remember Cassandra told me they were involved shortly before I arrived in L.A. I had no idea they had a working relationship, too.

"She's getting a plan together to manage his crisis. Don't be surprised if you get bombarded with reporters or see a strange car parked across the street with someone spying on you."

"You're scaring me."

"Reporters out here are hungry for the next big headline. Photographers get paid thousands to snap photos of you doing ordinary things. Around here we call them *paparazzi*."

"Who are some of Anna's clients?" Cassandra asks.

"You won't get me to name drop." Mona flips her hair.

"*Awww*, come on. You can tell us." Cassandra says.

Mona glares at her then rolls her eyes. "Anyway, as I was saying, now that JB is in the headlines, they are going to be targeting you, and believe me, they have their ways of finding things."

"Be careful what you throw in the garbage," Ursula adds.

"No way. They sift through your garbage?" I ask.

"Welcome to Hollywood," Mona announces.

I can't finish the other slice of pizza before a sudden dreadful feeling comes over me. It gives me a chill.

# Sixteen

I consider myself a fearless person—after all, it takes nerve to get on stage and perform before thousands—yet I've never been so scared to where I'm afraid to leave my house. I beg the girls to spend the night with me for fear that if I open my patio blinds, I'd see a strange person there with a camera, snapping my every move. If I happen to go to the front door and look through the peephole, I'll see a shadow lurking on the other side. When I'm not performing, I usually like to hang out on the beach. Will I still be able to relax without someone filming my every move?

"How do I handle this?" I ask Mona.

"I'm a model and an actress, not a publicist" is her response.

"But you're my friend."

"As your friend, I'm telling you to be intentional about where you go and what you do."

"No such thing as privacy anymore," I say.

"JB was already popular before he announced his decision to go pro, but the minute he got on television and made it official, he became fair game. Now they want to find out everything about this basketball sensation. Who he's dating? Aye, let's check her out. What makes her so special?"

"Sounds like you got this all figured out."

"I interned with my sister because I thought I wanted to do this."

"Why didn't you?"

"It's a glorified garbage collector. Let's just say I prefer being out front because a face this gorgeous can't be behind the scenes."

"Your sister works with JB? She makes sure his image is clean?"

A smiles flashes across Mona's naturally pink lips, like she's privy to a secret she'll never let me in on. "We're talking JB. Hotshot basketball playboy."

I sigh and sink back into my pillow, feeling like Little Red Riding Hood and getting swallowed up by, *How crazy is this? A wolf*, which happens to be his nickname.

"And how did you manage to get him so caught up? He lost all sense of reality and took that plunge without a second thought."

I lie there quietly in bed next to her, thinking of the moments I spent with JB, listening to music, creating music, watching live performances to music, and how together we get lost in the music. Music connects us in ways only we understand. I think he loves that with me he can escape basketball and engage in something else he loves.

"It just happened" is my response.

"You think he loves you?" she asks, and the expression in her eyes is a mixture of pity with a hint of envy.

"Yes," I answer.

"When did you guys start dating?"

"It was more like hooking up."

"How many times did you hook up?"

"More than once."

"You hooked up while you were with Gregory?"

"He was in Europe. I didn't hear from him. What was I to think?"

"So, you and JB hooked up?"

"Yes."

"And now you're in love?"

"Yes."

"When is the baby due?"

"March."

She is quiet as I imagine she's soaking up all the information I just told her. Ursula and Cassandra are asleep on the sofa bed in the living room. I see daylight from the behind the blinds. I don't want to be afraid. I don't like it. If I want to be locked up inside, it's something of my choosing, not because I'm afraid of what someone will say and report to fit their narrative.

"My daddy's a minister. The headlines are trying to ruin his name."

"It justifies an old cliché: Preacher's kids are the worst." She laughs.

"No we're not."

"Yes, you are."

"Speaking of minister, my daddy is probably in his study reading about God's amazing grace."

"I'm Catholic. Remind me: Who is God again?" She chuckles.

I don't laugh. She notices and stops.

We are face-to-face on our pillows, and other than JB and Gregory, I've never been this close to anyone else in bed. I feel she understands me and the craziness that has now become a part of my life. We're silent. I feel her hand touch my stomach. She's gazing into my eyes with the same energy and intensity that JB gives and what Gregory use to give me.

"I'm not into girls," I hear myself tell her.

"I know," she responds.

"I just need someone to hold me right now, and you just happen to be a girl."

We burst into laughter until we are in hysterics. I feel tears rolling down my face. I look and see Cassandra and Ursula standing in the doorway wiping sleep from their eyes.

"What's funny?" Cassandra is still groggy.

"We want to laugh, too, dammit," Ursula adds.

I stop laughing. "I just want to be held right now."

"*Awww.*" Cassandra slides into bed next to me and gives me a hug.

"It's going to be okay, cousin," she tells me. She moves aside so Ursula can give me a hug as well.

"I just wish JB would call or let me know something," I say, feeling a bit anxious.

"I'm sure he will," Mona says.

"You think he's going to jail?" I ask.

"I don't know," Mona answers.

"If that were so," Ursula says, "these jails would be overflowing because there are a lot of guys in this town who are currently committing or have committed statutory rape."

"And how do you know?" Cassandra asks. She's now curled up at the foot of the bed with her head resting in the palm of her hand.

"Guys, promise you won't tell anyone outside this room," Ursula begins.

My heart starts beating rapidly, anticipating the news she's about to reveal.

"I was seventeen and Harry, my comedian friend, was twenty-seven when we met."

"Did he know you were seventeen?" Cassandra asks.

"I don't know. I never told him."

"He knew," Mona adds.

"They all know," Cassandra responds.

"The news reported that I was a concert pianist. What's going to happen to my career now?"

"I don't remember them showing your face, but if the television and the newspapers report your father and they make the connection to you..." Mona shrugs after that.

"It's hard enough for women pianists to gain a level of respect.

It's even harder when you're Black. I don't want these symphonic orchestras to judge me and not want to work with me," I hear myself crying.

They all embrace me.

"Maddie, take a deep breath and exhale." I feel air flowing from Mona's lips.

Cassandra goes into my bathroom and returns with tissue.

"Think you'll be okay to go to lunch with us?" she asks.

"No," I respond before using the tissue to blow my nose.

"Don't tell me you're going to sit here all day with the blinds closed," Ursula says.

"I will if I have to," I answer, and I turn to Mona. "Weren't you the one who told me I had to be intentional about where I go and what I do?"

"I did, but damn you need to eat," Mona answers.

"I have no intentions of leaving, thank you," I tell her.

They leave me alone. In my room is where I remain with the blinds closed.

\*\*\*

It's after midnight when I hear a constant tap on the door. I recognize it, but I look through the peephole just to make sure it's who I think it is. I open the door, and we rush into each other's arms, feeling his hands circle my back, feeling my hands grip his shirt with strong, firm hold. He rushes me inside, closing and locking the door behind him. I see his hair is cut low, and there isn't a single trace of hair on his face. He looks seventeen. We kiss. He stops kissing me and kneels to kiss and hold my belly.

"I can't stay, but I needed to see you," he says.

"What's going to happen to you?"

"I don't know, Maddie." He holds me tight.

"Can you go to jail?"

"I don't know."

"That is insane."

"I warned you. It's crazy out here."

"Are they following you?"

"Who?"

"The press."

"They always follow me."

"Can you make them stop?"

"As long as they don't physically harm me, it's their right."

"You know if they've followed you here?"

"No one was following me. Are they following you?"

"No. How did they know about me?" I ask.

"Who do you talk to?" he asks.

"What do you mean?"

"Do you have people you talk to regularly?"

"Just Cassandra and my friends Mona and Ursula. Then there's Aunt Mary, Uncle Frenchy, Daddy, Gilda, and Caleb. Only other person who knows about us is Gregory."

"Gregory? Who is that?"

"My ex-boyfriend."

"Your ex." He nods quietly. His mind appears to be sprinting.

I recall the last conversation I had with Gregory. Outside of my family and friends, he's the only one who knows about me. JB's quiet, still holding me close. "The press got me looking rapey. They're really pushing the issue of statutory rape. If we stay together, they say I'll run the risk of going to jail plus lose out on the draft and a spot in the Olympics, but I can't walk away from you."

"I don't want to be the reason you lose everything."

"I can't walk away from you," he repeats, kissing my lips.

"My daddy wants you to call him."

"You think he's awake? I really need to talk to him." He looks into my eyes.

I get the phone and dial his number. I listen as it rings about six times before he finally picks up sounding groggy and disoriented.

"Daddy."

"Maddie?" I can tell he's turning on the lamp light and scrambling to get adjusted in bed. "Is everything okay?"

"I'm fine. I have JB here with me. I know you wanted to talk to him."

"Yes, absolutely. Put him on."

I give JB the phone. "Hello, Mr. Richardson. I apologize, it's late. I wanted to say how sorry I am that your name is in this."

The phone is loud, and I can hear Daddy just as well, as if he were talking to me.

"I'm no stranger to smearing and character assassination—it's par for the course as far as I'm concerned. However, I have a problem when it involves my daughter."

JB listens as Daddy continues.

"Her emotional well-being is placed above everything—that includes my reputation."

"I understand," JB responds.

"Are you working with a crisis management team?" Daddy asks.

"I am," JB answers.

"Are you confident they can get the job done?"

"Absolutely."

"I wasn't aware of the age of consent for your state. I know here in Texas, it's seventeen."

"I only know one way to make this right—that's why I want to talk to you and get your blessing," JB begins.

He reaches for my hand. It's clammy. It's never felt like that before. I notice his leg is shaking.

"I want to marry Maddie," he says. I see his Adam's apple bobbing and sweat beads forming. He squeezes my hand, totally unaware he's doing it.

"That is the right thing to do," Daddy answers.

"I love her." JB takes my hand and kisses it. "She's real. I need that right now."

"She's an incredible human being," I hear Daddy saying. "You won't find a more loving, a more genuine, a kinder and more generous spirit. Now she's a lousy housekeeper—and we're partly to blame for that. We've always had help, but anyway, I digress."

"I need your blessing, Mr. Richardson," JB says.

"When you get a moment, I want you to open the bible and turn to the thirteenth chapter of First Corinthians, beginning with the fourth verse all the way through to the eighth verse. When you fully understand its purpose and believe and declare it over your lives, then you, JB, have my blessing."

He swallows. "Thank you, sir."

"Before I go, I want you and Maddie to get together and say these words, 'No weapon formed against us shall prosper.' Repeat it enough until you believe it. Amen?"

"Yes, sir," JB says.

"Good night, or should I say good morning," Daddy says, "and yes, I am aware that it's one a.m., and you are at my daughter's house. Let God's Word manifest in all areas of your life. You want to do right? Stop fornicating until you say those vows and put a ring on her finger."

JB takes a deep breath.

"Now that's love," Daddy says before he hangs up.

JB wipes away the sweat beads that have formed on his forehead and around his nose. "You heard that?" he asks.

"The part where you want to marry me, the part where we read the bible, or the fornicating part?"

"All of it," he answers.

"I did."

"So?"

"Yes. I'll marry you."

He leans forward to kiss me. It's sweet and gentle and soothing. "I have to get a ring to make it official," he says. "Your daddy says to stop fornicating. I haven't heard that word in a minute."

I'm wiping tears that won't stop streaming.

"I love you," he whispers, kissing and wiping away tears, "and I've missed you."

"I know."

"Now your daddy has me curious."

JB walks to my bookshelf and searches until he comes across my leather-bound bible. He grabs it and joins me on the sofa. I turn on a lamp light as he opens it and sees the picture of my mother.

"Wow," he says, pausing to admire it. It is a black-and-white photo of my mother on her wedding day. I've been told I have a heart-shaped, angelic face just like her. I have her almond-shaped, amber-colored eyes, her button nose, and her full, pouty lips. The dress she wore was vintage lace with a wide petticoat. She's looking away. Maybe Daddy was nearby and caught her gaze.

"That's what I say when I open it, too," I tell him.

He holds the picture up next to my face. "Twins," he says before proceeding to flip through the bible.

"You remember the chapter and verse?" I ask.

"No, but if I look it up in the index, I'm sure I'll find it."

"It's called a concordance, and there's lots of verses in the bible about love."

"You want to call him back?" he asks with a sly grin.

"I think I know which one he's referring to," I say, helping JB flip through pages. "He said First Corinthians."

I flip until I arrive at the passage. "I think this is it."

JB starts reading. "Love is patient, love is kind and not jealous; love does not brag and is not arrogant. It is not proud. It does not dishonor others, it is not self-seeking, it is not easily angered, it keeps no record of wrongs. Love does not delight in evil but re-joices with the truth. It always protects, always trusts, always hopes, always perseveres. Love never fails."

He nods. "Love is patient." He places the bible on the coffee table and falls back on the sofa. "I've been patient fifty-six days, fourteen hours, eleven minutes and twenty-two, twenty-three, twenty-four seconds."

"You've got it down to the seconds?"

"If I love you, I've got to be patient, right?" he asks.

"It's in the bible," I respond.

He sighs, clearly frustrated.

"I want to be patient, but I miss you so much," I say to him.

The looks we give each other are sometimes just as stimulating and fulfilling and intimate as the act itself. He has dark, penetrable, expressive eyes. His lips are parted, and now that he has no facial hair, he has a sweet, boyish charm. He's written about the way I look at him when we kiss. Now, my eyes are closed, and instead of his lips, I imagine a chocolate, strawberry, and vanilla ice cream swirl served on a sugar cone in summer during the heat of the day. Right now, I savor the taste of his lips just like I savor the sweetness of the ice cream.

\*\*\*

I finally get a TV with a VCR just to watch and record JB's games. I listen to sports commentators talk. "Trouble's brewing with star athlete JB who didn't suit up for tonight's game." I hear a second commentator announce, "What a phenomenal player on the court. Off the court, he's facing a bit of a challenge in his alleged involvement with an underage girl."

They cut to highlight footage of JB on the basketball court. He dribbles, he leaps after a ball into the stands. He dunks the ball in the goal, and the crowd erupts into spontaneous cheer jumping out of their seats.

"This 'SC program must prove they can perform without their leading scorer in the game. Who knows when he'll be able to play?"

I'm feeling nervous and anxious. JB doesn't really talk about it other than his public relations team is gathering information to present at a press conference.

Now the press is following me. After my doctor's visit, Gilda and I walk outside, and the press is there with their cameras and microphones shoving them in my face asking me questions. Gilda waves them off, but they trail us to the car.

"How long have you been in a sexual relationship with JB?"

"How many months pregnant?"

Once we're inside the car, I still hear them barraging us with questions. The sound is muted once the engine starts. Instead of dropping me off at home, I ride with Gilda to the hotel suite, which she's now made her home as well as her office. Hours later, JB and I are the lead story on the six o'clock news. They are showing Gilda and I when we were leaving the clinic earlier that day. Gilda's hand shields my face from the cameras. Still, all I see is the striped chambray jumper dress I was wearing.

"This madness is going longer than we anticipated," she says.

With so much happening, I haven't had much time to concentrate on my upcoming D.C. and Philly performances. One orchestra is focusing on the works of Liszt while the other is showcasing Tchaikovsky. I have musical scores to look over. Although I'm familiar with works from both composers, there are pieces I need to revisit and hear how they sound during practice.

"How long do you think I need to stay here?" I ask Gilda.

"Give it a few hours. By nine o'clock, they're tired usually," she responds.

She sits next to me on the sofa. "I'm putting together your portfolio for Juilliard—got deadlines looming."

"Already?"

"Absolutely. We've got to meet them if our plan is fall enrollment."

I feel a kick, and it seems the baby is doing slow stretches. At one point, I feel hiccups.

Gilda orders us room service. While waiting for the food to arrive, we go over numbers. She's transparent, always showing me what she spends on my behalf. She has a ledger with receipts. Even her stay at the hotel comes out of my budget. We wrap up the finance part of our meeting just as the food arrives. The staffer does a double take when she sees me. She opens her mouth about to speak but quickly changes her mind.

Later that night, we leave the hotel to arrive home and see a few reporters on the street in front of my townhouse.

"How do they know where I live? The house isn't even in my name?"

Pulling up, she turns off the ignition. "Sometimes it's the people in your circle. Who do you think is leaking your business to the press?"

I am totally speechless. I didn't think I had those kinds of friends. Sometimes Mona and I don't see eye to eye, but I don't think she would do anything to destroy me. Ursula has been nothing but sweet and supportive, even signing her name to the lease. She wouldn't. Cassandra does talk a lot, but at her very core, she has the biggest heart, and I know for sure she wouldn't stoop to this level.

We get out of the car, and they start yelling questions. I notice the neighbors turning on porch lights.

"Are you and JB still having sexual relations?"

"Did you know he could face jail time if convicted?"

"How would you feel knowing your involvement with him could land him in jail?"

Once inside, I have only the lamp light on in my bedroom. Gilda sits on the sofa while I take a shower, and when I return, she's curled up on the sofa asleep. I want to play my piano to drown out the stillness and to get my mind off the madness. Instead, I walk in my bathroom and repeat, "No weapon formed against us shall prosper, no weapon formed against us shall prosper."

# Seventeen

A circus describes the level of press and frenzied energy inside the L.A. Sports arena. I'm a ball of nervous energy sitting with a front row seat next to Gilda. Tons of camera people and reporters from the major networks are gathered. There is a stage with a table clothed in the school's colors and logo. I see JB along with his parents, Anna who is his PR person, and a guy who looks like the coach of the team enter the stage. JB pulls out a chair for Anna, who sits next to him. Next to her are Judy and James and the coach of the team.

Anna, dressed in a gray designer power suit with her hair done in a chignon, adjusts the microphone to speak. "Why?" she begins. "Why?" she asks again. She pauses and gives the room a moment to think.

"Who JB chooses to love should not be a public matter. If we were in Nevada, this wouldn't be an issue, which brings me to my question: Where is the crime? What is it about these two whose ages are less than four years apart that's driving us to the point where we are now? JB is an honor student with a 3.2 grade point average, he's an all-American, he's the leading scorer for his team, he's a member of a prestigious fraternity who prides itself on community service, he is a leader who rallies his team in clutch situations. To scandalize his name and his good record is akin to burying him alive."

I see JB reach for a glass of water, drinking it in one swallow.

"Ask yourself, is it worth it to ruin his name and all he's accomplished? Will you, the court of public opinion, be the cause for his destruction if he's charged with a crime? Let him play ball," she says, pausing again for dramatic effect.

Camera lights flash, and there are continuous rounds of clicks from the constant wounding of film. I sit dressed in a gray tunic maternity top paired with a stretchy A-line skirt. I'm trying to remain poised and calm. JB wanted me here. I had my reservations about coming for my own privacy, but that quickly went out the window. JB is given the opportunity to speak.

"I just want to play ball," he begins. "To get to this level has always been my dream. I want an opportunity to beat the odds—pursue my dream of playing pro ball. I don't want that taken away from me."

He's calm and cautious, measuring his words while camera shutters open and close like wings flapping on a flock of birds. "If it's not too much to ask, on behalf of myself, my family, my coach, and my team that you please respect our privacy. That's all I have to say." He pushes away the microphone. We make eye contact. He mouths the words, *I love you.* A warm, cozy feeling consumes me, and I find myself mouthing the words right back to him.

Anna whispers something to JB before saying something to the others on stage. At her cue, they all stand and exit the room. Reporters from major networks, cable news networks, sports networks, newspapers, and sports magazines bombard them with questions.

"Your team is on a three-game losing streak. You think your personal matters off the court may be the reason?"

"Coach, will you allow JB suit up for the next game?"

"Will this hurt his chances of getting drafted?"

A short time later, I meet with him and his family after the press conference in a private area, shut off from media exposure.

We embrace, and it's soothing and gentle and somewhat intoxicating how he melts in my arms the minute he sees me. I look, and there's Paul, his friend and frat brother, with his handheld camera. He and JB greet each other with their secret handshake.

"I had no idea," he says to me, and his eyes go directly to my growing belly. I don't know quite how to respond. I feel at this point I don't owe anyone an explanation. Judy and James enter chatting with the coach. JB introduces me to his coach. Other than small talk and pleasantries, we don't exchange a lot of words. Judy gives me a warm and loving embrace.

"Hi, stranger," she says, and I realize it's been a while for us.

James and I hug, and that feels awkward to me. Anna enters the room on the arm of another older, distinguished-looking gentleman with wide glasses and a bushy mustache. He greets JB with the secret handshake, a clear indication they're in the same fraternity. While they talk, Anna looks around the room until she sees me. She walks with grace and confidence, and her body looks too perfect to be real.

She greets James and Judy then introduces herself to me. She clearly forgot I was a guest at her Halloween party, so I greet her like it's the first time for me as well.

"Just a typical day in Hollywood," she says. "It hails you then nails you."

"I see."

She studies me for a beat. "I tell JB don't worry. We're good if we control the narrative."

JB approaches and takes my hand. She smiles, reminding me a lot of her younger sister, Mona.

"JB was my first client. I was a senior; he was a freshman, and one night I went to a game and saw him play. He was a monster on the court. You remember how many points you scored?" she asks.

"I don't," he says.

"Fifty-eight. As a matter of fact, you had triple doubles—imagine a freshman with those stats, game after game. I said there's something special about him. He's what legends are made of."

Hearing her say these things about JB is impressive. However, I can't help but notice how they look at each other. I noticed it during the press conference, how attentive and caring her eyes were on him. Cassandra told me—and her words were—"they messed around." Now that's in the back of my mind.

The distinguished-looking gentleman with the bushy mustache and wide glasses catches her attention, and she excuses herself.

"Who's that guy?" I ask JB.

"We call him Moses. If you're in the wilderness, it's his duty to get you to the promised land. You want him on your team."

"Who's all on your team?" I ask.

He smiles and bites his lip. "You. You're my top pick. You're my only pick."

"I'm glad you corrected that."

He gives me a smug grin with a wink. Anna and her companion with the bushy mustache and wide glasses invites us out to lunch. I learn he is an attorney who made a name for himself advocating for victims of police brutality.

"I am my brother's keeper." He says to me. "If my brother is in trouble. It would be the same as if I were in trouble. And if you know me you must know how I feel about trouble." He didn't elaborate, but judging his tone and from JB's "Moses," reference I get the sense he has the power of persuasion.

It is utter chaos, getting through throngs of press and maneuvering through traffic. Not to mention, waiting for a decent table. During the lunch, I'm fighting sleep and a headache when the waiter removes the silver cover to my entrée. I see a small box made of felt underneath.

I glance at JB who's now sweating. He wipes his face with his dinner napkin.

Everyone at the table pauses and watches in curiosity. I grab the box and open it. Inside is a shiny engagement ring. Tears rush my eyes. I'm nervous as he removes the ring from the box and gets down on one knee. Paul hurries and grabs his camera. Other patrons in the restaurant stop eating to observe.

"Will you marry me?" he asks.

"Yes," I respond.

He slips the ring on my finger. Now that I'm pregnant, I don't have the cute and dainty fingers I used to. Pregnancy has them swollen, and the ring barely makes it on my finger.

We kiss. The next day a headline reads, *Star-Collegiate Athlete Gets Engaged.*

\*\*\*

The timing of my engagement couldn't have been more perfect as Gilda and I are off to Washington, D.C., for my performance with the National Symphony Orchestra. On the flight, I notice her looking at my ring and then at me to get my reaction.

"What? You don't like it?" I ask.

"He didn't do too bad," she answers.

"But—" I hold it out to examine, sensing she has more to say.

"He's trying to do the right thing. I commend him for that."

"But—" I repeat.

"Why are you trying to put words in my mouth?"

"Do you think this is happening too fast?"

"As you mature, you see with a sixth sense. It's called intuition. It's beneficial to your emotional well-being. I, like you, get consumed with the men we love. We're attracted to their charismatic nature, finding ourselves in competition with the things they love, convincing ourselves to be secure yet harboring insecurity when they're not around or in the company of other beautiful, powerful women."

I listen quietly as she continues. "At seventeen, you are at the crossroads. You don't think like a fourteen-year-old, but you haven't lived long enough to experience heartbreak the way a thirty year old would."

I'm picturing her words, hearing them and what she's really trying to say.

"I understand the attraction, believe me I do. He's driven, he's fun-loving, engaging, and out of all the girls in the world, it's you he wants to spend his life with."

The thought makes me smile, and the following thought makes me wonder if his motive for proposing has to do with what I read in the article. In California, once married, you avoid facing statutory rape charges.

"Don't be foolish. Use your intuition. Men like JB and your father are surrounded by temptation. Your father claims his faith keeps him strong, and I pray to God that is the case, yet I'm not saying what he won't do—after all, he's human with needs, which brings me to my next point: a man's needs. He needs admiration and respect. He needs sexual fulfillment. He needs a home that offers him peace and respect. He needs you to stay attractive outside as well as inside. Last, he needs to have something in common with you, something that he can associate you with, something he enjoys."

I think of our love for the piano, and it brings a warmth inside as well as a smile to my lips that Gilda notices. She stops talking.

"What did I say to make you smile?" she asks.

"Just thinking about JB and how much we love music."

Something out the window catches her eye. I look, and the evening sun has just set over the horizon somewhere on our journey to D.C.

You never know how good you are until someone brings it to your attention. I just do what I'm supposed to do and make every effort to do it to perfection. My mother used to quote this: "Be the labor great or small, do it well or not at all." I think of her words when I'm rehearsing, and I really put it to use when I'm performing. I perform Liszt's "Hungarian Rhapsody No. 2," and I swear every time I play it, I discover something more enchanting and beautiful. It transforms me to a place—a happy place—that I never want to leave and dread when the song ends. I perform Saturday and Sunday nights dressed in black proudly wearing my engagement ring, seeing its diamonds sparkle under the stage lights, when my fingers tickle the keys like magic. D.C. owes me nothing.

The following week is Philadelphia, and their orchestra is one of the best in the country. Rehearsals are intense, and a couple of times, I excuse myself to use the restroom. The baby rests on top of my bladder. I perform Tchaikovsky's "Piano Concerto No. 1 in B-flat minor," and when the French horns sound off and the rest of the orchestra chimes in, I play, sometimes with my eyes closed, and sometimes I smile and sway with the orchestra. I love when the violins strum along. I imagine us on a raft on a rugged river riding the waves. I listen to the clarinets and mimic their intensity and subtleness, and then I imagine Tchaikovsky playing along with the orchestra—all of it feeds my performance. After thirty-six minutes, I finish and take my bow. The conductor takes my hand, and together we bow. Hearing the applause ring through the music hall gives me goosebumps and makes me incredibly sad to know that after tonight I don't know when I'll be able to get on a stage and feel that energy again.

\*\*\*

I arrive in Houston after being gone six months. The Christmas tree is decorated with ornaments, some of which were handmade from when I was a little girl. I walk up and touch it. Memories of making ornaments with my mother. Seeing her pictures throughout the house. Going upstairs to my room and lying across my bed, seeing my room as I left it six months ago. I open the closet and see clothing I can no longer wear. I look in the mirror and turn sideways. My pregnancy is no secret. Everyone knows.

"When did they finally stop camping out at church?" I ask Daddy.

"I haven't been really paying attention," he says, relaxing in his recliner reading a book titled *Beloved* by Toni Morrison. I notice his Bible and other literature stacked on an end table next to him. The television is off, and the flames from the fireplace produce a crackling sound when they lick the firewood. Except for his housekeeper who lives in a detached house, Daddy lives alone. It's a little too quiet. JB is back to playing on the team after sitting out a couple of games. I don't know if the engagement got him off the hook or Anna and "Moses" did major persuasion behind the scenes. Whatever the case, JB has a game today, but we won't see it here in Houston. I sit on the opposite end of Daddy and open my list of things I want for my wedding and my baby shower. I still need to find JB a ring. At some point JB and I will need to go to Nevada because California requires you to get a parent's consent, a court order, and blood work. Nevada only needs Daddy's consent. Daddy nods off in the middle of our conversation with the book on his chest.

While cleaning out my purse, I notice the tape JB recorded for me. I go inside my home's studio where my piano and stereo are and put the tape inside the player and get cozy on the window seat. The first song, "I Need Love" by LL Cool J reminds me of the morning inside the pool house. The melody is catchy, and hours later, I'm playing it on the piano. Prince's "Venus de Milo" is one of my favorites. It's a piano instrumental with lush orchestration. I see why JB chose it.

Usually in the days following a performance, a representative from an orchestral company will contact Gilda, and from there, other performances are booked. Not this time. Not a single phone call.

"Maybe because it's the holidays and people are on vacation," I tell Gilda when she comes over for dinner.

"Holidays hasn't stopped bookings in the past," she says.

But I think I know the reason. They've been watching the news; they've been reading the papers and magazines. They've connected me to JB and Daddy, and now they want no parts of me.

# Eighteen

It's New Year's Day. JB and I are standing in a room with views of the Sierra Mountains somewhere in Nevada between Reno and Lake Tahoe. Daddy does double duty, walking me down the aisle and officiating. I'm wearing an ivory-colored gown with a veil, carrying a bouquet of red roses. JB and I light unity candles in memory of my mother. Our wedding party is small. Cassandra is my maid of honor. When I told her I was getting married, she had nothing to say.

I remember her telling me, "Only a fool would be crazy enough to marry JB."

The same was said of Caleb, JB's best man. From the start, he was never in favor of us together. I took away his partner in crime. With me and a baby in the picture, the dynamic has changed. I didn't want a courthouse wedding, so Gilda found a ski retreat in the Sierra Mountains. The ceremony only lasts twenty minutes. We kiss, take pictures, eat, and dance our first dance to Michael Jackson's "I Just Can't Stop Loving You." JB and I are anxious to start our honeymoon early. We only have two days to celebrate. He's still in the middle of basketball season, and this is the only extended block of days off before the next game.

Our suite is large. I walk out on the terrace, and although it's dark, I see a glow from the majestic snowcapped mountains. The air is cold and crisp, and I notice my breath ascending into the darkness. It still doesn't seem real. I turn and see JB lying near the edge of the bed, a smile slowly emerging from his lips.

"Come here. Let me help you out of that dress," he says.

I close the glass sliding door to the balcony and sit next to him on the bed. He slowly unbuttons my dress. I close my eyes as I feel him kiss the ball of my shoulder. He whispers in my ear, "I don't care if we never leave this room."

I feel the fabric of my dress fall just at the top of my belly. He rubs my stomach, holding me close, kissing the nape of my neck. I turn my face to meet his kisses, gazing into his eyes.

"You're *my* husband now," I tell him.

He nods and says with a boyish grin, "I am."

Saturday morning finds us cozy and warm. I feel safe. Looking out at the terrace, it's daylight, and snow is falling. He grabs the remote and flicks on the television, channel surfing while singing the theme song to *Scooby Doo, Where Are You!*

"You still watch cartoons?" I ask.

*"Cheeuh."* As he scrolls through the channels, the glare from the television light reflects in his eyes. He stops on a channel, and we see *The Smurfs*. We watch quietly.

"*The Smurfs* remind me of Dee," he says.

I am thinking about her, too. "I miss her," I say.

"Yeah," he responds.

"Why don't we go see her mother when we get back to L.A.?" I say to him.

"Let's do that. I wanted to get something for Dee's siblings for Christmas, just didn't have the time," he says.

"Her first Christmas without Dee. I remember the first Christmas without my mom."

I feel JB's lips brush against my forehead.

"I wouldn't wish that feeling on anyone," I say.

"Dee would've made a really pretty flower girl," JB says.

"I know," I reply.

We had no flower girl and no ring bearer. It didn't make a difference to me. We have love, and everyone who was there saw it.

Afterward, during the toast, where we all drank sparkling white grape juice, James and Judy stood to say a few words. They both agreed they never knew or even recall hearing JB sing until he started hanging around me. Caleb said the same thing. Throughout the evening while talking with others, we'd steal glances at each other, and my heart melts now as it did months ago when he bites his bottom lip and winks at me. I'm in awe and captivated when a song plays and he sings along with it, sometimes acting out the words, sometimes getting me to dance and sing along with him.

"What are you having for breakfast?" I ask him.

"You" is his response.

"You're so silly."

"I want crepes à la Madeline." He showers me with kisses.

We eventually order room service. He turns off the television and turns on the stereo, getting his attaché with his collection of tapes. We listen to "I Want Your Sex" by an artist named George Michael. "I Want Your Sex" is the recurring theme, one of those songs that gets stuck in his head and often blurted and sang at random times. I hear him singing it in the shower. He sings it before and sometimes during the act. I think I heard him singing it while standing on the terrace.

We listen—or attempt to listen—to the entire tape by an artist named Keith Sweat. He has a nice song called "Make it Last Forever." JB is really feeling it along with the song "Right and a Wrong Way" and another song called "How Deep is Your Love."

I brought my staff sheets, and we get inspired, stopping sometimes to stand on the terrace for fresh air and stare out at the scenery. All that covers our bodies is the duvet from the bed and hotel house slippers on our feet. We're sticking out our tongues, tasting snowflakes. He's gentle and attentive, making sure I don't slip and fall.

The walls in our suite appear to be solid between the loud music and the sounds we make. I'm really hoping they are. At one point, we get dressed and go outside just to kick around in the snow. He lays down and makes a snow angel. Next, we build a little snowman with pebbles for eyes and a twig for its nose. He gathers a ball of snow and throws it at me. He finds it funny. Now we're having a snow fight. Even with leather gloves on, my hands are still freezing. We stop and laugh. It feels so good to laugh. It feels even better when we are back in our room.

We order more room service and watch more television until he presses his face against my stomach and gently rubs my belly.

"If it's a boy, what are we going to name him?" he asks.

"I don't know," I answer.

"Let's name him Jabari," JB suggests.

"Jabari?"

"Yes. Hollywood and I were talking. He says names should have meanings. He told me in some African countries, they have ceremonies just to name the baby."

"I think I remember reading something like that," I reply. "Jabari? What does it mean?"

"Brave," he answers.

"Jabari sounds strong."

"And if it's a girl?" he asks.

"I don't know. I was thinking of using my mother's name, but Evelyn sounds old fashion when you think about it."

"What about Melody?" JB suggests.

"Melody?"

"Yeah, Melody—we love to make music. Plus, a melody is what you and I created."

"Clever," I respond, rubbing his hair. It's cut low, so it feels like the fine bristles of a soft brush when I run my hand across it.

"Jabari if it's a boy, Melody if it's a girl," he says.

"I agree, but what's the middle name?" I ask.

"We've got more than enough time to think about it," he says.

"I'm so happy here with you," I say.

"Yeah, kind of wish we had more time," he says. "There's so much more I want to do."

"What did you have in mind?" I ask.

He looks at me and smiles. "A lot," he answers.

A lot is putting it mildly.

\*\*\*

When we get back to L.A., we stop in the Jungle to check on Dee's mother, Felicia. The neighborhood gives you the feeling you really are in a jungle with banana trees. I've never been in a jungle, but I imagine it's scary and you tread lightly because you don't know what's lurking or what's going to pounce on you. JB knocks on the door, and when it opens, a guy appears wearing a blue plaid shirt and khaki pants. He sizes JB up with his piercing eyes.

"I'll be damned," he says as his stare softens. "JB, what the hell—"

"I'm looking for Felicia. Is she home?" JB asks.

"You the third person that's been here looking for her." He glances at me with curious eyes before he proceeds to tell JB. "She moved, but if it's sticky green you need, my partner in the next building got you. He in Apartment One."

JB nods and backs away. "I'm good," he says to him before he turns and looks at me, shaking his head. Once inside the car, he turns on the ignition and puts it in gear. I look out the window at the apartments, watching them disappear out of view.

"Last thing I need is a headline reading I was in the J's looking for weed." He shakes his head.

"Is that what he meant?" I ask.

"Yep."

"You think Felicia sold drugs?"

"The father did. That's probably why he's still locked up."

"What do you think happened to Felicia?" I ask.

"We'll never know," he says.

The following night, he has a basketball game. I arrive with Aunt Mary, Uncle Frenchy, and Cassandra, and we have seats behind the team's bench. The atmosphere in the arena is charged with music from the band. The cheerleaders get everyone on their feet with their routines. An announcer's voice has the arena energized when he calls out the names of each player from the team. "At forward, six-eight junior from Harvard Prep Academy, JaayyyBeee." JB runs through a line of his teammates, which includes Caleb, slapping high and low fives. He is projected on a JumboTron screen that looms over the center of the arena. The crowd's boisterous roar, the spirited music, the energy makes my blood race and gives me an adrenaline rush and a high I know all too well. The team huddles. I can see the coach in the center talking to the players. They clap and break away from the huddle before approaching the court. It's my first basketball game, and I feel nervous. My teeth chatter as if I'm playing. JB rubs each hand on the bottom of each of his sneakers and gets into position. The referee throws up the ball, and USC gets possession, with JB's teammate and friend Jake dribbling the ball down the court.

"I still can't believe you're married," Cassandra says to me.

I smile because what I feel inside is warm and loving. Watching JB run up and down the court, the most random thought pops into my mind: *I've seen him naked.*

There are moments in the game where I'm biting my nails. I'm holding my stomach because the baby is kicking and stretching, obviously feeling the crowd's energy. JB's running and gunning, I see sweat pouring. It drenches his body. I want him to notice me. I want him to see how much I'm enjoying watching him doing what he loves. Despite his efforts, the team still loses.

The crowd boos. I hear people cursing. I overhear someone say, "If JB got his head out of his ass and into the game, maybe we'd start winning."

I wait until JB completes a press conference, answering questions about the game with some reporters going off the script and asking him about our personal life. I meet him in a waiting area when he's finished. He doesn't say much, and I give him space to think. During the ride, he's quiet and in deep thought.

When he parks the car and we get out to approach the townhouse, I notice the front door is open. JB holds me back and gives me the keys.

"I need you to wait for me in the car," he says.

My heart pounds.

"What's happening?"

"Go sit in the car." His voice is agitated and edgy.

I do as I am told. Minutes later, he walks out and sits inside looking as though he's just seen a ghost.

"What?" I ask.

"Someone burglarized the place."

"You're kidding."

He drops his head, pursing his lips in anger. I notice his fists are balled.

"Can I go inside?"

"I don't want you to."

Before he says anything else, I'm out of the car, and when I enter, my knees buckle at the sight. My piano is damaged, like someone took a hammer and beat the keys. Papers are scattered and shredded. I run into the bedroom to check to see if my mother's jewelry is missing. Her rare saltwater pearl necklace, purchased by my grandfather when he visited Japan, is gone. My compositions—my life's works from the time I was twelve, my thoughts, my emotions—are scattered into shreds. I fall to the floor. I feel JB grab me and sit me on the couch. He dials 9-1-1. The pain is so much, I'm screaming. I'm sure the neighbors hear it, but I don't care. He's trying to keep me calm while he's on the phone, but it's just making matters worse.

When the police arrive, JB gives them a statement. After they leave, he tells me to gather my things, and we spend the rest of the night sleeping in his old waterbed at home with his parents. My night is restless.

JB holds me. "You can have my songs," he says, trying to kiss away the pain.

When I awake from a brief rest, the reality that all my compositions are lost is too much for me. It's like losing my mother. It hurts that bad.

Judy taps lightly on the door before entering the room. When she sits on the bed, it makes a swooshing sound.

"Maddie, JB has a nine o'clock class. He told me to tell you as soon as he can, he'll be back to check on you."

"What am I going to do now?" I'm holding the pillow, squeezing it for dear life.

"I know it's easier said than done, but you've got to relax. Too much stress will make you go into early labor, and you don't want that."

"I'm sorry," I utter, adding all the incidents that got me to this point.

"I talked to James. Once you gather yourself, pack your things, move out of that place, and stay here."

"I don't want to impose on you and James' space."

"You're not imposing."

"I don't think James likes me."

"Why?" she asks.

"He says I'm a distraction."

"It's hard for him to accept the son he's groomed for success all these years had a momentary lapse of judgment. James created a Superman on the basketball court, but kryptonite weakened Superman—much like you, a sweet, innocent girl with a gorgeous face and stunning figure weakened JB."

"I don't want to get in anyone's way."

"Honey, truth to be told, James is hardly here. Let me tell you more about the basketball life: Once you get a taste of it, it's hard to get out your system."

"I see."

"James is always on the road, trying to find something that'll keep him tied to basketball—whether it be coaching, consulting, working in an office or commentating— getting in his way should be the least of your worries."

My thoughts drift back to the overwhelming feeling that all my work is destroyed. I'm afraid I'm not able to pour anymore of my heart into something for fear it could get snatched away and destroyed.

Judy offers to cook me breakfast, but I don't have an appetite. Very much, like all the other times, all I want to do is sleep. It allows me to not deal with the pain as much.

* * *

I talk to Gilda and tell her what happened.

"You have more music inside you," she tells me. "Your greatest song has yet to be written."

With that in mind, I set out to write. When I grab a tablet, a photo of JB and Basha falls out of it. I pick it up and see she's smiling wide at the camera as he's kissing her on the cheek. I'm wondering if this was taken before or recently. Soon my creative spark is replaced by my curiosity. JB's room is a shrine to all his accomplishments: trophies, medals, plaques, shoes, jerseys, and shorts. A gold diamond watch from a different university is still inside the box. On the shelf are albums, books, and old pictures. A net contains several basket-balls with autographs scribbled on them. I open the closet, and the smell of leather and teakwood is eminent. I run a hand over his suits and other outfits. I look down and see dress shoes, men's sandals, and sneakers. He has long, narrow feet. I pull a USC sweatshirt off the hanger and bring it up to my nose, inhaling his scent. My thoughts are overwhelmed with so much—pregnancy, marriage, the burglary, the baby shower, Dee's death, Rosie, and my impending registration deadline with Juilliard. Now I see how easily I can slip into madness, like the crazy, dead white men whose music and lives I've studied and performed.

I remain in JB's room searching for inspiration when I hear a constant tapping on the door, and he appears.

"How's *my* wife?" he asks.

The baby kicks, and I rub my stomach. "I don't know," I respond.

He kisses me. "I couldn't stop thinking about you in class."

"Judy says I can stay here," I tell him.

He nods. "Cool. I talked to my frat, and his dad sent some people over to repair the damages and clean up the place."

"I'm not going back."

"You don't have to."

"I don't feel safe there anymore."

"I get it." He thinks about something for a minute. "Any songs you want to salvage?"

"Maybe."

"Think you want to do it today?"

"Sure." Though I am reluctant, I get dressed and go.

When we arrive, a repairman is working on the door. Inside, I scavenge through the papers, trying to piece together my composi-tions. Whoever did this made sure I'd never be able to use them. All the piano keys are destroyed. I go to my closet and look closely. My designer tops and dresses and scarves have been doused in bleach and hung back up neatly. A sickening feeling grips me. I look and notice the mattress destroyed, fabric and cotton exposed; feathers spill out from the pillows.

I get on the phone and call Ursula. "Where are you, and how soon can you get here?" I ask.

"Are you okay?" she asks.

"No," I respond.

"What's wrong?" she asks.

"Everything. Where's Mona, do you know?"

"I think she's with Ruger."

"Do you have a contact number for her?"

"Yes."

"Call her and tell her to come here right away."

"Are you in danger?" Ursula asks.

"I don't know." I feel my voice catch.

"I'm on my way," she says.

About an hour later, Mona and Ursula arrive with questionable stares. They walk in tiptoed movements.

"What in hell—" Ursula begins.

Startled, they look around before sitting on the sofa, which I notice the arm has a knife rip and material exposed. JB walks down the staircase from the loft. Ursula and Mona both eyeing him.

"Hi, JB," Mona says.

He nods and sits at the base of the stairs.

"What's up?" Ursula asks.

"That's what we want to know?" JB begins. "Maddie and I were very private. Not many knew about us. Funny, as soon as we made it known to our friend circle that we were together, that's when the headlines started."

"And you think we started it?" Mona points to herself and Ursula.

"Did you?" I ask.

"No." She looks disgusted.

Ursula shakes her head. "You think I'm responsible for this?"

"Whoever vandalized this place knew that I loved music. Look at my piano...all my compositions—gone. Destroyed."

"We're sorry this happened to you, but we aren't the problem here, I promise," Ursula states.

"Mona, when did you see Gregory last?" I ask.

"I don't know—a week or so ago. You think he's behind this?"

"Besides you, Ursula, and Cassandra, he's the only one who knows I love music, and the last time I saw him, he wasn't too happy."

"When was that?" JB asks. The tone of his voice has an edge to it.

"November, right before Thanksgiving," I answer.

"Before Thanksgiving?" JB asks.

"I was at Cassandra's debutante ball, and I remember coming out of the restroom, and I saw him, and we spoke."

"Really? Is that all?" JB asks.

I look at all their reactions, and all three are looking at me anticipating an answer to JB's question.

"Yes." I feel myself suddenly getting in defense mode.

"Why didn't you tell me this before?" JB asks. His tone is still edgy.

Now, I'm flustered, like I've been keeping a secret that should've been made known to him. "I don't know" is my answer.

"He knew about us. He knows about your father and the church. Did you tell him about this house?" JB asks.

"No."

"I know it sounds strange, but it's hard for me to think Gregory did this," Mona begins.

"I agree," Ursula adds.

"Where does he live?" JB asks.

Mona and Ursula shift in their seats, looking at each other, searching for words.

"Listen, you have a lot to lose. Don't do anything rash." Mona holds out her hand.

"I just want to know where he lives." JB is calm.

"Sure you do," Ursula responds.

"You're not going to tell me?" he asks them before looking at me. "Maddie, do you know?"

The nerves in my body pulsate; the hairs on my arms stand. I only know how to get to his boat in Marina del Rey.

"JB, I promise you," Mona begins, "I've known Gregory longer than anyone here. He wouldn't do this."

"He could've hired someone," JB says.

"He's hurt, but trust me, he wouldn't do this," Mona says.

I think of my compositions and my mother's pearls and sit on the couch with my face buried in my hands. I want to confront Gregory, but I know doing that will only make the situation worst for JB.

# Nineteen

There are ten of us gathered before Paul's video camera smiling and saying well wishes.

I'm center in a Tiffany blue—my favorite color—maternity dress; a floral head wreath accents the curls cascading down my face. A photographer captures candid images of us. The pool area is decorated in Tiffany blue, and a table is set for ten. This time a staff is hired to cook and attend to us. We play baby shower games like guessing how many bubblegum balls are in a jar and how many squares of toilet paper it takes to fit perfectly around my growing belly.

"Anyone have advice for to the mother-to-be?" someone asks.

"I do," Judy begins.

She's sitting next to Aunt Mary. They are both holding their glasses of red wine. Judy looks at me, smiling. In the two weeks that I have been living with her, she's been teaching me how to cook and clean. Her words to me were, "Always make your home a place where JB looks forward to coming to." Although they could afford one, she never had a housekeeper or a nanny. Judy always chose to be hands-on. When James was out on the road with basketball, she learned how to fix and repair things around the house. She told me, "Most husbands appreciate you more when you're resourceful."

"Maddie, go easy on yourself. You won't always get it right," Judy says to me.

"Get rest," Aunt Mary adds. "Don't be afraid to ask for help."

"Don't compare yourself to other mothers," Gilda says. "You have your own journey, and no two journeys will be the same."

"Make sure you have a village you can trust," Aunt Teal says. "That's why Mary and Frenchy have me in their house to this day."

"In your eyes, your child never grows up," Judy says. "JB and Caleb are now twenty-one years old, and they are still our babies." She sips from her glass of wine.

Speaking of twenty-one, JB along with Caleb and the rest of his fraternity brothers spent the weekend celebrating his twenty-first birthday in Las Vegas. It was our first argument. I wanted *us* to celebrate his birthday, but Las Vegas was planned before we considered getting married.

I open gifts, grateful for the thought and consideration poured into each one. Earlier this week, Judy purchased a crib and bedding, and she's turned one of the spare bedrooms into a nursery. Of everyone, she's the most excited—more so than me.

Of my ten guests, only Judy and Aunt Mary are mothers. Gilda never wanted children. Aunt Teal never married or had children. Aunt Mary's assistant, Leah, never married or wanted children. Dr. Blue, my obstetrician, is married but doesn't have children. Mona, Ursula, and Cassandra all say it will be years from now before they even consider it.

I get home to Judy's that night with all the gifts assembled in the nursery. She shows me how to wash delicate clothing by hand, and I am amazed at her energy, despite her and Aunt Mary having had drinks and fits of laughter at the shower. I just knew she would come home and go straight to bed.

"Thank you for helping me," I say to her.

She just taps my hand and continues to fold baby clothes in

the nursery. She's painted it Tiffany blue. I sit in a rocking chair with Tiffany blue cushions and hold my belly, feeling kicks, turns, and stretches. At times, my belly stretches to the point it feels my stomach might rip open.

"James' mother helped me," Judy says.

"How long did she stay?"

"A couple of weeks. I nursed JB so I didn't get enough sleep because he ate every three hours for two days straight. I was so exhausted."

"Every three hours?" I ask, amazed.

"Yes, and when he finished, I burped him, and next thing you know, he's pooped his diaper, so I clean him, and it's time to nurse again, then I burp, then I clean poop—it's a continuous cycle."

"I see."

"Boys never stop eating and growing. By the time JB was in junior high, he was already six feet and eating cereal out a cake mixing bowl. We kept him busy with basketball during the summer months, otherwise he'd eat up everything in sight."

He'd be impressed to know that with Judy's help, I learned how to prepare a couple of his favorites, Filipino fried rice and Filipino Pancit with rice noodles and vegetables. But with all the cooking lessons and preparing for motherhood, I've neglected my music. I try to get inspiration, but there is none. I try to remember key chords and measures of my sunset composition but draw a blank. I sit before JB's keyboard, going through his notebook of songs, but they are only lyrics, and lyrics need a melody. I never thought I'd see the day when I'd run out of music. I listen to the tape of JB's love songs, hoping I can hear a note, a chord, a refrain, but nothing.

I'm still trying to process losing my compositions. I still have moments where I cry. Gilda and I talk upcoming concert engagements, it's been close to a month since my last performance, and still the phones are not ringing. There was an editorial written about my Philadelphia performance in a musical trade magazine. It stated, *Although this musical prodigy teen sensation encompasses the spirit of Tchaikovsky, it appears the demands of her personal life have taken center stage.*

How do they know about my personal life? I've never discussed it with anyone. Right now, at this this point, I am no longer motivated, nor do I have the energy.

"You need a hobby," Judy says to me. She plays tennis and goes bowling with her Filipino friends. "If you keep wondering what he's doing, it'll drive you crazy. Get in an activity that will keep you busy."

I notice James is gone most of the day, and sometimes he doesn't get home until late. I overheard him and Judy arguing one night. Because the door to their bedroom was closed, I couldn't make out exactly what they were saying, but I'm sure it had everything to do with him not being around. Then there's the phones. One line is separate and designated for JB and James' business. It never stops ringing. I can't get rest with the phone constantly ringing.

I go outside to the pool house and sit at the keyboard, hoping I can draw inspiration from something—a word, an action, an unforgettable moment. I think about our honeymoon weekend. I want to capture it along the theme of firsts—after all, that weekend, a lot of firsts happened. But not even a series of first-time activities is enough to get me motivated to pick up a pen to write.

\* \* \*

It is February 14, also my eighteenth birthday. At last, I'm officially an adult. No more needing permission from my daddy. I wake up crying and happy but also reflective. Since the day I discovered my pregnancy and getting married, the difference between doing adult things and being an adult can only boil down to a matter of days.

The team has lost more games than they have won, and I can't help but wonder if I am partially responsible for that. JB is the captain, and everything rests and falls on his shoulders. I try not to bother him. Sometimes he comes home to check on me, and we make up for lost time, but I can't help but wonder when he's alone and really has time to think if the responsibility of a wife and a baby become overwhelming. I know it does for me sometimes. He does a good job of hiding his true feelings on that, but I know deep down inside, this has got to be too much too soon.

I awake to find fresh flowers along with a note that reads: *What you mean to me is more than anything I could ever imagine. JB.* I see a red velvet cake and cupcakes with pink buttercream icing topped with strawberries. I try one cupcake, and it is rich and mouth-watering. It's so good.

I look outside and see JB pouring dog food into Smitty's bowl. He's wearing only shorts, which means he just finished his morning run. I watch him, and my heart flutters with anxious excitement, anticipating the minute our eyes meet and we say good morning.

He enters and finds me standing there.

"Happy birthday," he says.

"Thank you."

"How are you and my baby?"

I rub my belly. "We're fine, just happy to see you."

"Paul's coming around to take photos of us. Can you wear something really pretty?"

"Sure."

Paul usually does video. He did the video of our wedding, and we're still waiting for him to finish. JB tells me Paul takes his time because he is a perfectionist.

"Thanks for my cake and cupcakes. I tried a cupcake, and it was delicious, though I didn't smell anything baking in the kitchen last night."

"Mom didn't bake these. Can I try one? My hands are dirty." I pick up a cupcake and hold it while he bites into it. After chewing, he says finally, "Aunt Teal did."

My heart melts. "Of course she did."

I remove the liner from around the cupcake so he can finish it. "Mouthwatering," he says.

"Here. Have another one. I'll share it with you." I grab another cupcake, and together we savor each bite. Now our lips are covered with buttercream icing. We kiss icing off each other's lips before he picks me up and carries me to the room.

*** 

Paul arrives around noon with his camera equipment, setting it up in the living room.

He even has lighting equipment set up. I look at JB, and he's changed into a white button-up shirt with a red bow tie and black slacks. I'm dressed in a red maternity jumper dress with my hair teased out with bangs.

"I'm capturing the love on this Valentine's Day," Paul answers. He aims at us. "Act natural—pretend I'm not here," he says.

JB kneels on one knee and presses his face against my stomach, holding me. I naturally rub his hair. It's still short and feels like a soft brush to my fingertips. Next, I'm sitting on his knee looking into his eyes. He puckers his lips for a kiss. I lean in with my eyes closed and feel the tenderness of them against mine.

"Perfect. I like it. That's it," Paul says while his camera clicks away.

We go outside and pose with the dog, Smitty. I sit on a lounge chair with JB behind me, and Smitty sits at my feet.

"Look at my brother," Paul says from behind the camera. "Wife, baby, and a dog."

"Isn't that the American dream?" JB asks.

"That's what they say," Paul answers. "Oh, I think, we'll need some shots around a grand piano."

"Nearest grand piano I know is at Caleb's house," JB answers.

"Do we have to now?" I ask, feeling a little hungry.

Judy and James left shortly before Paul arrived, saying they were going to brunch.

"Yeah, why not? It won't take long," JB says. He helps Paul gather his camera equipment before we leave.

When we arrive and the door opens, I am bombarded with shouts and cheers. "Surprise." I see a banner with *Happy 18th Birthday, Madeline* decorated in red and pink. Paul is there to capture it all, this time with his video camera. So many faces in the room. I am so overwhelmed.

Aunt Mary hugs me. "It's official," she says.

"It is."

We celebrate. I open gifts. I pose for pictures with JB, James, and Judy, then Gilda, then with Aunt Mary and Uncle Frenchy. JB gets on the piano to play a song.

"I wrote this after a game, on the bus ride to the airport." He starts to sing.

*People tell me we're moving fast*
*They say our love won't last*
*What do they know?*
*How can they conclude?*
*All I know is there is no substitute*
*The love I have for you is true.*
*Our love is the truth.*

I'm fanning back tears as he's singing, serenading me, making me feel special, like no one else is in the room, but the place is crowded. When he's finished, I give him the biggest hug and kiss.

I talk to Daddy who says he'll fly into L.A. tomorrow to take me out for a celebratory lunch.

Evening comes, and JB is gone back to campus, and I'm alone again. Yes, I signed on the dotted line for this.

# Twenty

These aren't the Braxton Hicks contractions of which I experienced episodes shortly after my eighteenth birthday. These contractions feel like the real thing. At my last visit, Dr. Blue said I was already five centimeters dilated. The cramping and pressure come every three to five minutes. I feel wetness between my legs. I think my water broke. I notice JB isn't next to me. Since the season ended, he's been in the pool house with the towel over his head and headphones in his ears. The press, the university, James, and everyone is talking about the rough season they just had. Now he's doubting himself, wondering if his decision to turn pro was premature. I overheard him and James arguing.

"If you'd kept your head on straight, you'd be working on building a better team for next year or consider transferring to UCLA."

Why did James say that? I almost thought they would come to blows. I always give JB space. I understand the pressure a person can put on themselves. It isn't easy, too, when James holds up his championship ring and tells JB, "This is what you get when you keep your head in the game."

I'm still without inspiration. Sunsets are taken for granted. I don't appreciate the beauty of the color in the skies like I used to. I've got an audition in New York at the end of March for Juilliard.

My thoughts tell me, *Why do you need Juilliard? You had a three-month guest pianist obligation with L.A. Phil, you performed a weekend with the National Symphony Orchestra and a weekend with the Philadelphia Orchestra—all because you were exceptional at what you do. No number of hours at Juilliard can confirm that.* Then I think, *You've always dreamed of studying at Juilliard. You promised yourself you were getting in. Don't let that dream die.*

With the contractions coming as quickly as they do, along with the strong intensity of the pain, I feel as though I am dying. I can't understand for the life of me how some women choose to endure the pain multiple times. I can't, which is exactly what I say to a nurse once JB and I arrive in the labor and delivery room, "Please give me something for the pain."

JB watches me, trying to maintain his cool, but I can see it in his eyes. He's so scared. An anesthesiologist enters the room with tools. I'm told to sit up and remain still, but a strong earth-shattering contraction hits, and I cry, reaching out for JB to come and hold me. He kneels until we are eye to eye. I drape my arms over his shoulders.

"Now, I will need you to remain still," the anesthesiologist tells me a second time.

I pray he's administering the epidural effectively before another contraction hits. I hold on to JB's shoulders. We're still looking into each other's eyes. I feel a tear roll down my cheek.

"I love you so much," he whispers.

"I love you—" My lips are trembling.

I feel the sting from the needle being inserted into my spine followed by another strange sensation that feels like hot wire. Another contraction hits. This time I squeeze JB.

"Hurry, please," I say.

"Remain still." The anesthesiologist's voice is soothing.

When he's finished, nurses are on hand to ensure I don't feel a thing, and minutes later, I don't.

"You just had another contraction," a nurse tells me.

"I did?"

They hook me up to a monitor that tells them when my contractions occur. Once JB and I are alone, he sits next to the bed and holds my hand, kissing it.

Judy is outside with James. I'm relaxed to the point where I can call Gilda who's still here in L.A.

"The baby's coming," I say to her.

"I'm on my way" is what she says.

I call Aunt Mary. "The baby's coming."

"We're on our way," she says, and I imagine *we* includes the rest of the family.

My next call is to Daddy.

He answers. "I'm making plans to get on the next available flight" is what he says. "I'll see you in a few hours."

As I get off the phone, I see on the monitor that I've just had another contraction, but I don't feel a thing. I can't imagine enduring excruciating pain without the aid of some pain relief. I've experienced enough contractions to know it's not something I'm willing to put my body through.

"You're handling this good." JB kisses my hand, holding it against his lips.

"I really can't feel a thing." I am so relaxed I'm nodding off.

I awake later to Dr. Blue's voice. I'm a little disoriented.

"Hello, Maddie," she says. Her voice is bright and cheerful.

My mouth is dry and tastes like cotton. I simply wave, feeling the effects of the anesthesia. JB is now asleep on the sofa next to the bed, unfazed by movements from the staff and their voices. Dr. Blue examines me down there. I can't feel a thing.

"You've dilated to nine centimeters," she says to me.

As she's saying that, a sheet is placed over my lower half, and my legs are placed into stirrups. I look at the florescent lights in the ceiling and think, *Ready or not, it's coming.*

I hear JB stirring on the sofa, and now he's awake.

"Hi," Dr. Blue says to him.

He and Dr. Blue exchange pleasantries, and soon he is by my side, holding my hand and kissing it. His eyes are red and moist.

"Can you see anything down there?" I ask him.

He looks. "No, not yet" is his reply.

I check the monitor and see contractions coming more often than before.

"JB, are you ready?" Dr. Blue asks.

JB takes a deep breath and exhales. He squeezes my hand.

"On the count of three, Maddie, I want you to push." Dr. Blue says.

It's strange that part of my body is numb, but I'm pushing as hard as I can.

"Push, push, push," she tells me.

I'm pushing, willing it, giving it my all, although I can't feel a thing. I'm pushing and pushing for several minutes until I hear Dr. Blue say, "Just one more push."

I look at JB. He's staring at something. His eyes are wider than I have ever seen them. "I see the top of the head," he says.

I reach between my legs, and I feel wetness. The texture is sticky.

"Okay, Maddie. Push, push, push."

I push, raising myself up from the pillow until I am exhausted. Falling against the pillow, I hear a loud cry and what sounds like a suction, and the room is filled with the sound of a newborn baby with powerful lungs.

"Congratulations, Mom and Dad. It's a girl," Dr. Blue says.

JB stands, shaking his head in disbelief as the baby is placed in my arms. Nurses wipe and towel away fluid from her body. She glistens under the hospital lights. She is so incredibly beautiful. Her face and mouth are round and perfect. I kiss her hands, holding her close to me. I can't believe my eyes. JB sits on the couch. His shirt is pulled up to cover his face. I see his shoulders shaking; I hear him crying. My first time seeing him this emotional. He quickly composes himself and wipes his eyes.

"Dad, please." I see Dr. Blue hand him a pair of scissors to cut the umbilical cord.

The baby's still crying, and I feel my emotions and everything fill up inside me. Now, I'm crying, a combination of relief mixed with the reality that JB and I are responsible for another life—one we unintentionally created.

"What's her name?" a nurse asks.

"Melody," JB and I announce simultaneously.

"What's the middle name?" the same nurse asks.

JB and I look at each other. We both shrug.

I say, "Evelyn."

He says, "Judith."

The nurse looks confused, unsure of what to write. Then I think about Dee and how much joy she brought to us when she was alive.

"Melody Delight," I tell the nurse. I glance at JB, and he approves.

"Melody Delight it is." The nurse writes.

A second nurse takes her to weigh and get her footprints. She's fussing, not liking it. Her cries are loud and clear. She stops crying once she's swaddled up and placed in my arms. JB kisses her head. She coos and sucks on her fist.

"She's gorgeous," he says.

"Would you like to hold her?"

He looks nervous. "Sure."

"Please don't drop her," I beg.

"I know how to hold a baby," he says.

He picks her up and holds her in his arm. He's in awe, amazed.

"Hi," he says to her.

I hear her coo and gurgle, breathing through her nose.

The staff cleans me up and moves me out of the delivery room and into a private room. James and Judy are already there waiting. Judy is excited. James is more laid back.

I'm holding Melody. She's in and out of sleep. I can't stop looking at her, watching her every movement—her eyes open and dance. I imagine she's trying to figure out this new environment she's in.

"She's gorgeous," Judy says. "She's got my mother's eyes."

"She has grandmother's entire face," JB says.

Judy walks over to get a closer look. "She's absolutely beautiful." Then she starts speaking in a high-pitched tone. "Hello. It's me, Lola. Welcome, sweetie."

James walks over and stands behind Judy. He places a hand over her shoulder. "And this is Lolo," Judy continues in her high-pitched voice.

"Lola and Lolo?" I ask.

"Yes. Grandma and Grandpa," Judy answers.

James turns to JB who's been quiet. "She's here. She's a beauty. Clean your shotgun."

JB takes a deep breath and exhales. "I've got to get one first."

"Act fast. She'll be sixteen and dating before you know it."

The dynamic between James and myself still feels odd. If JB or Judy isn't present, we don't have much to say to each other. I've been staying with them for two months, and when James is home, he's either in his office or inside his bedroom with the door closed. As much as Judy likes to cook, it's rare he sits with the rest of us, and I know it has everything to do with me and JB, like he can't come to terms with the idea that JB has desires and interests outside of basketball.

"May I hold her?" Judy asks.

"Sure."

She gently takes her out of my arms and holds her, smiling. "You're going to get spoiled," she sings.

James smiles. "Your granny will spoil you rotten," he adds.

"Lolo says he's not spoiling you, but we know better," Judy says to Melody.

James looks cheerfully into her face. "It's going to be hard not to," he says.

Gilda, Aunt Mary, Cassandra, Caleb, and Uncle Frenchy arrive. Daddy arrives later that evening. Aunt Mary and Gilda cry when they see Melody. All of them say she looks like my mother. Daddy just holds and rocks her, walking around the room, talking quietly, and praying over her.

She's quiet, but I know she's hungry. When it's just JB and me alone, I unbutton my gown and lie her upon my chest, and she instinctively finds her way to my breast, latching on and feeding. I feel milk drip from the other breast, wetting my gown. JB notices. He hurries to grab a hand towel out of the bathroom, and I use it to stop the dripping.

"I'm going to need a new gown," I tell him.

"Where is it?" he asks.

"Inside my suitcase."

He goes to the closet to retrieve it from inside my suitcase then helps me change out of it, all while Melody's nursing. The sensation is relaxing. JB snuggles up next to me on the bed.

"Doesn't seem real yet," he whispers.

"I know."

"She's so beautiful, Maddie."

"She is."

He sings the song "Isn't She Lovely."

Melody's cheeks are moving. She stops, and her eyes open.

"She recognizes my voice," he says.

"Keep singing," I tell him.

Her eyes are still open, and she appears alert, staring into space, listening to his voice. I imagine it's soothing to her ears. I notice the ring on my finger and the gold wedding band on JB's finger, and I pinch myself and think, *Wow, this is crazy. I am eighteen. I am a wife. I am a mother.*

Two days later, I'm wheeled out of the hospital with Melody in my arms. I place her in the car seat and buckle her up. JB drives while I sit with her in the backseat, staring at her round, plump cheeks and her hair full of soft ringlets. Once we arrive at JB's parents' house, I take her straight to the nursery and close the door when I hear the phone ringing. It's the only quiet place in the house. I sit in the rocking chair with her in my arms. I'm exhausted but still excited because this is new. The first time I changed her, her poop was like tar. I find out from a nurse this is called meconium, and it's normal.

Judy was right. All babies want to do is eat. Melody nurses every three hours. I gently rub her back so she burps, and minutes later, I hear her poop, so I clean her up, place her in her crib, and sit in the rocking chair to get some sleep only to awaken hours later exhausted. I take her and nurse, and while doing that, I try to rest my eyes, and then I realize I have an audition in New York a week from today. *What do I do?* Melody is not due her recommended vaccinations until she's two months old, and I don't really want to bring her on an airplane. I can't imagine driving, but if that's what it takes to get to the audition, I might consider it.

I rented a breast pump from the hospital, and while Melody's asleep, I pump. I manage to pump enough milk so Judy or JB can feed her while I rest. When Cassandra sees me, she gives me a hug.

"Maddie, you're a mom."

"I know."

"How do you like it?"

"It's a lot. I'm so tired."

She's quiet. "I hear baby's grow fast," she says finally, making light.

"I need to practice for my Juilliard audition next week, and I'm too exhausted to think."

"You can do it blindfolded."

"Think I should fly or drive?"

"Fly. Have you driven from L.A. to New York?" Cassandra asks.

"No."

"Trust me, you definitely don't want to drive."

"But I want to take Melody with me."

"Oh. I don't think you should do that either."

"I can't leave her here. She eats a lot, and I'm afraid she'll drink all the milk I pump."

"How bad you want to get into Juilliard?"

"Do you have to ask?"

"Well, if it were me, I'd start pumping, then I'd make flight arrangements."

"Gilda did it about a month or two ago. I was trying to find a way to tell her I want to drive instead so I can bring Melody."

Cassandra walks to the crib where Melody lies asleep.

"She is so pretty," she whispers. "I'll babysit for a couple of hours."

"Just a couple? Thank you, cousin," I say to her.

"Where's your husband?" she asks.

"At the gym."

"Does he help?"

"Sometimes."

"What does that mean?"

"He'll change her sometimes. Because I nurse, he really doesn't get a chance to feed her."

"Last week, Kyle was in town for spring break, and we hung out with Gregory."

"Okay."

"He named his boat Sea-Thing."

"Sea-Thing?"

"It's a play on words. Since you guys broke up that's all he's been doing: seething."

"I think he had something to do with breaking into my townhouse and destroying my piano and all my compositions."

"Gregory wouldn't do that."

"How are you so certain?"

"Gregory is annoying, and he can be an ass, but how you described the way your apartment was destroyed and your mother's pearls were stolen...Even the way you described how your clothing was bleached... That doesn't sound like something he'd do."

"Who else could've done it?"

Cassandra shrugs, then she covers her mouth. "Omigod, you think Basha could be behind this?"

*She never crossed my mind.* "But how would she know where I live?"

"People in L.A. have their ways of finding out things about you."

When JB and I talked about the end of his and Basha's relationship, he just said they went separate ways and she was okay with that. Now I'm left wondering.

# Twenty-One

JB and I take Melody to the pediatrician for her first checkup. He tells us she's lost two pounds but don't be alarmed. It's typical for babies to lose the weight, which he describes is fluid from being inside the womb. We leave the pediatrician's office and run into Dr. Blue's nurse Rachael in the hallway. Her smile shifts when she sees us. She clears her throat. I glance at JB who glances back at me smiling with only his eyes.

"Hi, Rachael," I speak.

"Hi, Maddie." I notice she has a weird expression, and her cheeks are flushed. She becomes more upbeat when she sees Melody in my arms. "She's beautiful."

"Thank you." I turn to JB. "This is Dr. Blue's nurse, Rachael," I tell him.

JB's hands are buried in his pockets. "What's up?" he asks.

It seems like a minute before Rachael answers with, "You're really killing it with this family guy act." Her tone makes the hairs on my arms stand.

"You two know each other?" I ask.

"We do," she says, and how she says it gives me reason to believe there's more to it—very much like the situation with his publicist/ Mona's sister, Anna.

I turn to JB for an explanation.

"Rachael and Basha are best friends," JB says to me.

When I look at Rachael, she smiles. It appears forced. "At least you moved on," she tells him before she says to me, "Best of luck with everything." She walks to an elevator that just happens to open as she steps in, and another person steps out.

Once outside in the car, it's hard to compose myself. I haven't had much sleep, plus I've got to fly to New York to audition for Juilliard.

"Of all the nurses in L.A., my obstetrician's nurse happens to be your ex's best friend?"

"Small world. Yeah, I know," he says.

My breasts are engorging, and the sensation isn't pleasant.

"What did she mean by family guy act?"

"I don't know. Why didn't you ask her?" is his reply.

"Because I'm not the one with unfinished business."

"What are you talking about?"

"You think Basha's over you?"

"To be honest, I don't care what she thinks" is his reply.

"How can you say that about someone you were in love with?"

"Maddie, I'm looking to get to the next level, and I want to surround myself with people who are real. Basha was in love with the attention more than she was with me. I liked her because she was fine as hell and she had a good head, but then you came, and what I love about you is that in your eyes, I'm not a hotshot baller. I'm regular JB."

"What about you and Anna?"

He looks at me and frowns. "Where is that coming from?" is his reply.

"The way she looks at you—the way you look at each other."

He's driving, and I can tell his mind is racing because I see his temple jumping. "What did you hear?"

"What do you mean?"

"Her sister told you about us?"

My heart is pounding. "Is it true?"

He looks at me and doesn't say a word.

"You slept with Anna?" I ask.

He nods.

"When?" My eyes brim with tears.

"Before you and I started."

So, what Cassandra said is true.

I wipe away a tear. Angry at myself, fully aware of what I was getting into when I married him. Why should I be upset? Anna, Basha, all the other girls—they are the past. *He's with me now.* I'm remembering lyrics he wrote:

*I threw away the black book*
*Don't need it anymore*
*You made me fall hard*
*The minute you walked through the door*

"How many more have you slept with that I know?"

He doesn't answer but keeps his eyes on the road, looking in the rearview mirror and over his shoulder while weaving through traffic.

"Answer me."

"It doesn't matter. I'm riding with you now, and that's forever—'til the wheels fall off."

I hear him, and right now, I want to believe him. I close my eyes and try to bear the pain—the piercing and throbbing. I'm cramping. It feels almost as if my uterus is contracting again. We get home, and I sit in the rocking chair, and at that moment, I hear a whimper from Melody, and relief for me comes when she nurses at my breast. I purchased a nursing bra, so a round breast pad over my other breast prevents it from leaking, but then it still becomes saturated with breast milk, and I switch Melody to the other breast and close my eyes. When she's finished, I burp her and put her down in her crib, and I have about an hour or two to practice on my piece for my audition. It's hard to focus. I can't stop thinking about Basha, Anna, and the look on Rachael's face. I imagine they are somewhere laughing at me saying, *She thinks she's got herself a real family guy. Oh boy is she in for a rude awakening. He'll tell her how special she is and how much he loves her until the next girl comes along and blows his mind.*

\*\*\*

It's agonizing leaving Melody. I must've pumped nearly two dozen bottles of breastmilk, and I still don't think it's enough. Judy's keeping her, and she assures me Melody will be okay, but I'm not. I pack my breast pump and a bag with enough clothing to last two days. I'm crying when Gilda arrives to pick me up for the airport. I'm holding and kissing Melody.

"Stop worrying. She's in good hands," Judy tells me.

I'm standing in the doorway holding Melody. She's asleep.

"Okay, Maddie. I've got her." I place Melody in Judy's arms.

I wipe away a tear and load my luggage into the car with Gilda. I'm sobbing on the way to the airport, and I feel my breasts leaking, even with breast pads.

"It's okay." Gilda's voice is soothing.

The flight is five hours, and twice I use the restroom to relieve my breasts, expressing milk from them, crying, sitting on the toilet, looking at my reflection in the mirror. I look at my face and see puffiness and dark circles from crying and lack of sleep. She's eight days old, and although I have Judy, Gilda, and Aunt Mary around to help, there are times I'm overwhelmed. *How will I do this without them?* I still haven't had a good night's sleep. I remove breast pads drenched in breast milk, replacing them with new dry pads, praying for the minute I can get a decent night's rest.

For my audition, I'm praying my breasts behave. During the musical theory exam, they tighten and swell on me again. I almost give up. I enter an auditorium where there is a panel of four, and

I introduce myself to each one. I tell myself to relax and be composed as I sit before the piano. I have a couple of pieces in mind, but instead, I am told to play the fourth movement of "The Hammerklavier Sonata, Beethoven Opus 106, Piano Sonata Number 29 in B-flat Major."

*Wonderful,* I think, a sonata, almost like the Schumann toccata, with which my digital technique must be impeccable. How I remember certain pieces is going back to the feeling I had when I first heard them, What was I doing and who was I with? I first heard this piece when my mother played it. I think I was ten. I studied her technique. It was flawless. The clarity of the sound was rich. I remember in my mind the room transforming into a sea of cumulus clouds that seemed to float past us and me thinking, *This has got to be the greatest song ever composed.* I play it—the interpretation that I remember—and execute it. They interrupt me around the five-minute mark, but I wish they hadn't. I could've played the rest of the fourth movement.

I sit patiently while they write and critique quietly amongst themselves, their whispers hushed in the vast auditorium. My breasts are burning. It's like someone is holding a lighted match to my nipples. Then I'm told to play Liszt's "La Campanella." Remembering famed concert pianist Martha Austin playing this piece, I begin, hearing the notes seemingly dancing and the fine acoustics in the auditorium. I play, and this time they don't stop me—they allow me to play the entire piece.

Then it hits me: *How can I play pieces of movement from other composers and I can't remember the melody to my sunset composition?*

"You will be notified by mail" is what I'm told.

Remembering last time, I got a letter about a month later telling me I got accepted. This time feels different, though. Gilda and I rush back to the hotel room where I pump, and I call Judy to see how Melody is doing.

"She's a big eater like her daddy."

"How many bottles are left?"

"She has thirteen. When do you come home?"

"First flight tomorrow morning, but if you think I need to get there sooner, we can fly out today."

"She'll be fine. Just hope you're not delayed on your scheduled flight time."

I get emotional. "Thank you, Judy."

"You are not crying," she says, pretending to sound upset.

"Have you talked to my husband?" I ask.

"No. Though I hear he and James are flying to Kansas City to see some college games. Did he tell you?"

"No" is my response.

"Just wait until I talk to him," she says. "Give me your number so I can tell him to call you."

I rattle it off.

"How did the audition go?" she asks.

"I think I did well. I'm just anxious right now."

"If you were good enough to get another audition, you are good enough to get in," Judy says.

"You're right."

I hang up with that thought in mind.

Passing the time in New York City is agonizing. Gilda and I go to dinner and a Broadway play. We see Tennessee Williams' *A Streetcar Named Desire*. When we return to the room, I notice the message light blinking. I check it. It's JB saying how much he misses me and he's excited for my audition.

The following morning, Gilda and I fly back to L.A.

I go over ways I could've improved, thinking of different scenarios. It's enough to make my head spin.

When we arrive at Judy's and I see Melody awake, the craziest thought comes to mind: *What's going to happen if I don't get in? What if JB doesn't get drafted or selected for the Olympic team?* That statutory rape situation is still in the back to some people's minds. I just saw a report about JB on ESPN.

Once Judy leaves, I retreat to the nursery and rock Melody in my arms. She's alert, cooing. At times, she's smiling at the sound of my voice. My eyes are blurred with tears. I'm consumed by an overwhelming feeling. If Juilliard doesn't work, then I'll need Gilda to book me concerts. I'll need to get a passport for Melody and possibly a work visa for myself in case I'm booked out of the country. When I think Gilda's back at the hotel, I give her a call and tell her what I want to do in case things don't work out with Juilliard.

"Maddie, I understand you're anxious. Let's wait before we consider booking more shows."

"What if we miss out waiting on Juilliard?"

"Maddie, sweetheart, focus on Melody, and when you get a moment, see if you can get those creative juices flowing again."

With that, she hangs up.

I lie Melody in her crib and find a staff sheet and try to remember chords and keys to the sunset composition. I know I envisioned it in colorful patterns. Red, purple, then slowly fading to black with stars twinkling in the night. I spend a couple of hours on it, close to a creative breakthrough when Melody awakes. She's crying.

"Not now, baby girl." I'm hearing a note that I think will make the piece sound complete.

Melody's crying grows louder, and I pick her up to nurse. I pray, *God, give me inspiration.*

# Twenty-Two

Melody is crying again in the middle of me writing a new song. I zoned out for a minute, but it's hard to focus when her cries are loud and piercing. I look over and see her in the crib. Her tiny hands and arms are flapping, her feet kick and stiffen. I finally pick her up to soothe her. She smells my familiar scent, and she immediately turns her head to my breast, only crying louder, almost impatiently when I take my time to unbutton my blouse. Once her mouth is on my nipple, she stops crying and grunts almost as a way of saying, *It's about time.*

She's almost two weeks old, and already I see how much focus and energy it takes to care for her. I'm analyzing her cries, her poop, certain sounds she makes. I'm scrutinizing any change to her skin. Certain mannerisms I'm noticing—how she smiles in her sleep and her eyelids dance and eyes open at times. How she frowns for no reason then appears as if she has a few choice words for me.

I brush her hair. It is a layer of lose curly ringlets, very much like JB's hair before he cut it. I can tell she's going to be tall with long legs like her father. She's starting to look more like him with dark almond-shaped eyes. She even has his mouth. JB adores her. Before he left, he rarely placed her in her crib, instead holding her close to him, lying her on his chest. Now he's been gone close to a week—

meetings with the agent, meetings regarding the Olympics, training all day in the gym. Now he and James are in Kansas City. He calls me in the afternoon during a rare time where I'm resting.

"How is my favorite girl?" he asks.

"Who?"

"You. Who did you think I was talking about?"

"I thought Melody replaced me."

"She is a very close second, though—just by a hair," he adds.

"We miss you," I say to him.

"I miss my girls, too."

"When are you coming home?"

"Tomorrow."

"I'll actually see you?"

"Of course."

"Dr. Blue says we can't do anything for two to four more weeks," I tell him.

"That's okay," he responds to my surprise. "I'm not tripping."

Sometimes I find it hard to believe that he waits. My thoughts get the best of me, and I wonder with all the people—especially women—whom he encounters daily, does he get the urge to want them? Does he fulfill those certain urges? Like last summer when he fulfilled his urge for me inside the pool house. Who knows?

"Write any new song lyrics lately?" I ask him.

"No" is his reply.

"Have we run out of songs?" I ask.

"We're full of music. We could never run out of songs."

"But I feel blocked."

"It happens to the best of us."

"I've never dealt with this before."

"Consider this: You got pregnant, married, and gave birth within a year's time. Not to mention, you got shot at, house burglarized and vandalized, compositions destroyed and watched Dee's death."

"That's a lot."

"No shit, Sherlock."

"What if Juilliard doesn't accept me this time around?"

"Then it's their loss."

"You don't understand how bad I want this."

"I do. I understand how every moment you think about it, dream about it, you even write song lyrics to it."

I listen quietly as he continues. "You want it so bad that it happens."

I sigh, convincing myself to think positively.

"Remember this: *No weapon formed against me shall prosper.*" His voice is calm and soothing, I imagine him lying across the hotel bed.

I repeat it.

"You don't just say it, you believe it," he says.

"No weapon formed against me shall prosper." I say aloud.

"That's it."

"I want you to come home." I say to him.

"I am."

"Like now."

He chuckles. "Bye."

Immediately after I hang up with JB, the phone rings again.

"I love you, too," I answer.

"That's good to know. The feeling is mutual." It's Aunt Mary.

"Hello, Aunty."

"Maddie, how are you and Melody?"

"We're great."

"Good. I was wondering if Dr. Blue and I could stop by. We have something we need to share with you."

My heart sinks. "Does this have anything to do with Melody? Is she okay?"

"It has absolutely nothing to do with Melody, but we need to talk."

I don't like the sound of her tone, and now I'm anxious—walking back and forth to the door looking through the peephole, wringing my hands, watching the clock. It's three in the afternoon. Judy is out with her friends and won't be home until later tonight. Melody's been asleep for almost an hour and a half. I check on Smitty. He's asleep too. The doorbell rings, and I open it and give Aunt Mary and Dr. Blue a hug.

"How's motherhood been treating you?" Dr. Blue asks.

"I have my good and bad days," I answer.

"What kind of day is today?" Aunt Mary asks before she and Dr. Blue sit.

"So far, good."

"Where's Judy?" Aunt Mary asks.

"She's out. She won't be home until much later."

"I see."

"Well," Dr. Blue begins, "I came across some disturbing information regarding my nurse, Rachael, and another woman, who I later discovered is a friend of Rachael's."

"Do you know her name?" I ask.

"Does Basha ring a bell?" she asks.

"Yes. It's my husband's ex-girlfriend."

"Rachael and Basha have been leaking your personal information to the press," Dr. Blue says.

My heart drops.

"I've also been informed from another source they hired someone to burglarized and damage your property," Dr. Blue continues.

My ears are ringing, and I feel my chest rise and fall.

"This source reveals the ex-girlfriend was on a mission to destroy JB's character and derail his chances of getting drafted into the professional league."

I'm speechless, taking this all in.

"Rachael has been terminated from our system because she was in violation of the Privacy Act when she informed the press you were pregnant."

I'm shaking my head, still grasping the news.

"Six degrees of separation is real out here," Aunt Mary adds.

"What happens now?" I ask.

"The penalty is a fine and possibly jail," Dr. Blue answers.

"They stole my mother's pearls. They destroyed my piano and all my compositions." A sick feeling forms in the pit of my stomach. "They nearly destroyed JB's character, not to mention my daddy's reputation."

"How did they find out about Eugene?" Aunt Mary asks.

"Maddie is covered under her father's medical insurance. All of his personal information was on the paperwork he signed on the first visit."

I'm feeling a headache coming on.

"I will see that this is handled in the best possible manner and that there are consequences to such actions," Dr. Blue says. She turns to Aunt Mary. "In the meantime, I'm closing my office for an audit. There's no telling how many more of my patients' health records were compromised."

When JB arrives the following afternoon and he's settled in, I tell him. I've never seen his face turn a deep shade of red.

"She tried to destroy me," he says. His chest rises and falls, the anger brewing under his skin.

"Please don't do anything. Dr. Blue says she'll handle it."

"You don't understand how hard it was to sit in class and hear people laugh and talk about me."

I sit in his lap and wrap my arms around him.

"My teammates were tripping and telling jokes. It's not always easy to take the high road. Now the IOC is reviewing my status."

"Are those the Olympic people?" I ask.

"Yes. They've almost got a team assembled. I'm the only one whose status is still in limbo."

"Everything will work out," I assure him, massaging his temples with my fingertips.

"I was once considered the number one draft pick. The number one draft pick gets the biggest guarantee and the sweet endorsement deals. That's not happening for me anymore."

"Remember what Daddy said to us over the phone that night when you came to the townhouse?" I ask.

He doesn't answer.

"Did you forget?" I reiterate. "He said no weapon formed against us shall prosper," I tell him.

He looks at me. Stress is written all over his face. Yesterday he was motivating me. What a difference a day makes. I hear Melody crying in her nursery down the hall. I look at the clock and notice it's her feeding time.

"Come. Let's bond with her together," I tell him.

He follows me into her nursery. He checks her diaper to see if she's wet. She is crying at the top of her lungs. He picks her up and grabs a diaper from a nearby stack I keep on hand. He lays her down on the changing table. She's flailing her arms and kicking her legs.

"Daddy's got you, baby girl." He removes her wet diaper and wipes her clean.

I'm impressed he knows what he's doing. I'm standing nearby, shushing, watching him sprinkle baby powder on her private parts before he fastens her diaper into place.

"Did I do it right?" he asks.

"Perfect," I tell him before gathering Melody in my arms.

She stops crying the moment her lips touch my breast. In a corner of the nursery are a stack of decorative pillows where I sometimes sit to relax. We sit, and while Melody's nursing, he and I kiss—slow and passionately. Then I hear the sweetest voice:

*You are my refuge*
*My shelter from the storm*
*With you I feel safe*
*For you won't cause me harm*

He says this between kisses. I smile, feeling my heart overflow. I am amazed that once again, he improvises so beautifully from a place of vulnerability.

"She tried to ruin me," he says after a period of silence.

"She didn't, okay?"

"I'm not okay," he says, shaking his head.

"Please be okay for me."

He's looking away. I reach up and turn his face so that his eyes meet mine. "Don't even think about doing anything foolish."

He scoffs. "You have no idea how hard it is for me to restrain myself right now. If my frat, "Moses" hadn't been able to pull some strings, I'd be facing jail time."

"I understand, but please, think about me and Melody."

He relents.

"I cooked," I tell him, hoping it takes his mind off the Basha situation.

A smile slowly emerges across his lips.

"You're so sweet. That's why I chose you. You stay in your lane. You're not trying to be my publicist, you're not trying to be my agent, you're not trying to be a fan. You cook for me, you're loving. Your hair is real, your eyes are real, your lips are real." He palms my free breast. "This is real," he says, grinning, biting his bottom lip. He sends a sensual tingle all over my body.

Melody stops nursing, and I place a burp cloth over my shoulder.

"Let me do it," he says.

"You know what you're doing?" I ask.

"Why do you always ask me that?" he snaps.

"I'm sorry. I forget you're a super dad," I say in my best attempt to smooth things over.

"I've burped her before."

I place a burp cloth over his shoulder. He takes her from my arms and places her across his shoulder.

"Don't pat too hard. Be gentle," I tell him.

He gives me a look. "I know what I'm doing." He gently pats her back. I gently stroke her hair until we both hear her burp.

"There. Daddy's little girl is all good." He wipes her mouth before kissing her forehead. We cuddle, play with her, and rock her until she falls asleep. I look at her lying in her crib, and I still ask myself, *Is this real?*

JB and I enter the kitchen. Judy didn't help me, so I'm a little nervous. I remove the lid from the pan and show him what I prepared. He looks and studies it for a bit.

"Looks like Pancit with chicken," he says.

"Yes," I answer.

He opens a drawer to retrieve a fork, rinses it off in the sink before forking a piece of chicken, twirling noodles around it.

He takes a bite, and I study his expression, my heart racing. He's chewing.

"How long did you cook these rice noodles?" he asks.

I shrug. "Until they were soft."

He swallows and smiles.

"They're horrible, aren't they?" I shriek.

"I love you for trying." He stifles a laugh before bringing me close for a hug.

"I've ruined it." I feel tears.

"Maddie, hey, I'm not tripping."

I feel a tear roll down my cheek. He looks at me. "Hey. Stop."

I hear myself sobbing, releasing pent-up frustration from trying to care for Melody, not knowing whether I'll get into Juilliard, my destroyed compositions, messing up dinner.

I hear him sighing. "It's okay."

No matter how much he tries to comfort me, I still feel like a failure. It's deeper than a messed-up Filipino dish. It's missing out on an opportunity of a lifetime, one that I had been dreaming about all because I failed to use protection with JB.

"How about this: Let's try and cook this together? You feel up to it?" he asks, sounding upbeat.

I wipe my tears. "Okay."

"We'll do it this time without chicken." He forks a piece of cooked chicken from the dish I've already prepared and chews it. "Next time add salt and pepper."

"Okay."

"I appreciate you trying."

"Thank you."

"Let's get to work."

And we do.

# Twenty-Three

JB, Melody, and I are on a plane to Houston. Melody got her two-month vaccinations a week ago. I'm glad Judy was there to hold my hand. I cried, too, when the pediatrician's nurse administered her shots. The stinging sensation from the needle had my baby screaming. Her cries were distressing and heart wrenching.

We arrive in Houston, and the humidity hits me right away. Gilda who's since moved back to Houston is at the gate when we arrive. She picks up Melody who's awake out of her stroller and cuddles her close.

"Your daddy's in a meeting. Otherwise he would've been here with me." She smiles at Melody. "You are growing too fast, princess," she says to her.

"She's above average on her charts," I tell Gilda.

"Of course, she is." She glances at JB who's strolling alongside us, calm and relaxed. "First time in Houston?" Gilda asks.

"We've passed through maybe once," he answers.

"That's right. Your father mentioned he was from Tuskegee." Gilda's walking with Melody in her arms.

I told Daddy as soon as she was vaccinated, we were coming, and while we're here we'll get her christened. I've asked Aunt Mary and Uncle Frenchy to be her godparents. They are coming on a later flight. James and Judy are coming on a later flight as well.

During the ride, I'm pointing out landmarks to JB. We drive past Daddy's church. It's a grand modern building with a huge cross out front. It looks like a small college campus.

I show him the Catholic elementary school I attended from kindergarten to fifth grade.

"We weren't Catholic, but my parents liked the rigid structure," I tell him.

"My parents put me in Catholic school for the same reason," JB says. "It didn't help."

I glance at him, smiling. "Something tells me you were terrible."

"Was I," he begins. "You never know what cruel and unusual punishment is until you've experienced a Catholic paddle."

"You're saying the punishment didn't fit the crime?" Gilda asks.

"Miss Gilda, they carved holes shaped like crosses in that paddle."

"But you didn't answer my question," she says, laughing.

"No," he answers, "and we lived in Alabama then, so the nuns were swinging like Babe Ruth when they saw my black behind."

Gilda and I can't stop laughing.

We pull into the u-shaped driveway of the home I grew up in. It's springtime in Houston, so unlike the winter holidays, the flowers Mother had planted from long ago along with the roses are in full bloom.

Gilda has a tight hold on Melody. "Maddie, show JB your room."

JB follows me upstairs carrying two suitcases. Once inside my old room, he places them on the floor then walks over to look at a painting of me and Mother. She's sitting on a piano bench turned away from the piano, and I'm sitting next to her. I must've been six or seven because my feet barely touch the floor.

"Beautiful," he says.

My breasts are full. Gilda enters my bedroom holding a crying Melody.

"It must be feeding time." Gilda says when she places Melody in my arms before she turns and exits the room. I unbutton my blouse and sit on the edge of my bed to feed her.

"How much longer do you plan to nurse?" JB asks, picking up my high school diploma with its valedictorian seal.

"I don't know. Maybe until she's a year old" is my response.

"I thought you stop when they grow teeth."

"No. It's up to the mother when she wants to stop."

He walks to my desk and picks up a handful of mail. "You've got letters from Berklee College of Music, Curtis Institute of Music, Manhattan School of Music, Columbia, Barnard College."

"They're not Juilliard."

"You wouldn't consider them?"

I give him a look.

He doesn't say anything before lying across the bed.

Gilda taps lightly on the door before entering the room "I got this in the mail yesterday. I thought they would've sent this to California, but then I remembered the last address they have on file is here in Houston." She places an envelope in my hands. I read, *Juilliard, 60 Lincoln Center Plaza, New York, NY 10023*. My palms are sweating; my heart is pounding. Last time, the response came a month later. This time is two months. This can't be good. JB and Gilda look, waiting for me to open the letter. With Melody still at my breast. I open it and read aloud:

*Dear Madeline:*

*Congratulations! It gives me tremendous pleasure to inform you that the Juilliard piano faculty and the Committee on Admission have granted you admission to the **Classical Music—Bachelor of Music** program at the Juilliard School for the 1988–89 academic year.*

I'm holding the letter in my hands trembling. I feel tears pouring down my cheeks. I look and notice Gilda crying. JB sits up on the edge of the bed and holds out his hand to read the letter. I watch his eyes dance across the page. He gets to the end and looks at me with a big grin.

"You did it again," he says.

"I did."

He leans forward to give me a kiss. "Congratulations."

I look at Gilda. "I did it."

"I'm so happy for you," she says, wiping away her tears.

When Daddy arrives, I share the news with him. He holds me and cries.

"I hope you're proud of me," I tell him, wiping away tears.

"I am," he says.

"It means everything to me, knowing I make you proud."

"I'm glad you stuck with the plan."

"It was going to eat me up if I didn't."

"You know who else I believe would be proud of this moment?" he asks.

Minutes later, we're all in the car driving down the highway stopping once we arrive at the cemetery. I take my acceptance letter with me, and I forget about everyone else. I run to Mother's grave and fall, happy I got accepted, glad I did not give up on myself. I get a second chance, and this time I promise to make good on my opportunity.

Later that evening, I share my news with Aunt Mary and Uncle Frenchy when they arrive. Aunt Mary fans back tears.

"I don't expect anything less," Uncle Frenchy says. "You were born to fly."

I tell Judy and James when they arrive.

"I always knew," Judy says.

James nods. "You are something special."

Hearing that from James makes my heart dance. Seeing how he's always been—standoffish, suspicious of my motives, resenting the bond JB and I have and how fast it developed.

"She is," JB says, confirming it.

"You do well at that school," James says to me.

"I will."

Hearing all the lively chatter reminds me of the times when my parents entertained guests. Mother loved to have company over for afternoon tea and they sometimes ended up staying for dinner. For entertainment, she would have me play something on the piano. I show JB my studio, my black Steinway grand piano where I rehearse, and my upright Steinway with all my sheet music.

"Daddy's housekeeper does a good job with dusting. I haven't touched these keys since the winter break."

JB fumbles with a few keys before he finds the chord needed to produce a melody. I check out his hands and how he centers them on the keys.

"May I?"

I start to play my sunset composition, remembering the notes that I once forgot, allowing them to come back to me and flow through my fingertips. I caress the keys, tickling and courting them. I close my eyes, remembering certain sharps and the tempo. My fingertips are magic now, and I have absolutely no control over them. When I'm finished, I open my eyes and look at JB.

"What's the name of the song?" he asks.

"'A Melody of Sunset,'" I answer.

"Who's the composer?"

I smile. "Me."

\*\*\*

Gilda had my old christening gown dry cleaned. I was four months old when I wore it. I purchased a new christening gown to have on hand in case my gown was too big, but it fit Melody perfectly. JB and I along with Aunt Mary and Uncle Frenchy are standing before Daddy at the altar.

"Every day God sends us blessings in the form of babies," Daddy begins.

Melody watches Daddy while he speaks, cooing, moving her arms, and kicking her feet in the way babies at two months should.

"I remember when I first saw my granddaughter's image. It looked like a tiny seed. I said, 'Isn't God awesome?' Everything in life begins as a seed. Seeds need nurturing to grow to their full potential, very much like babies. Seeds become trees like babies become adults. It's up to us to make sure the foundation is good at the root so the branches can grow wide and strong."

Daddy christens Melody, sprinkling her hair with water before gently towel drying it, then he says a prayer before lifting her up before the church. They applaud. Daddy gives her a kiss before placing her back in my arms. I kiss her hands. She's awake. Her eyes are sparkling underneath the church lights.

"I love you, Melody. I can't imagine my life without you," I whisper.

She must understand because in that moment, she smiles.

\*\*\*

*June 27,1988*
*New York City, NY*
*11:42 p.m.*
*I realize my last journal entry was November before Thanksgiving. I wasn't married yet, and Melody was still growing. Today I met with two Juilliard professors for the upcoming year. They heard about my audition, how my interpretation of "The Hammerklavier Sonata, Beethoven Opus" left the audition committee in awe. They were impressed with my technique and flawless execution. One wanted to hear it, so I played it for him. I am looking forward to starting in September. Judy says she will stay with me*

for six months to help with Melody. JB knows for sure he's not the top draft pick, but hopefully he will be drafted.

Over the past months, the days have been full of surprises, starting with Cassandra's graduation gathering at her home. I was not expecting Gregory. He walked in with an attitude like he owned the place, dressed in the latest designer fashions, smelling like expensive cologne. I noticed Cassandra, Kyle, Mona, and Ursula get quiet and observant. I sat at the edge of the pool. He talked to Cassandra's other guests before he eventually noticed me. We made eye contact; no words were spoken.

Throughout the gathering, we managed to stay on opposite sides of the room. When I was leaving, I heard him say, "Congratulations," just as I was about to walk out the door. I simply turned around and glanced at him. "Thank you," I said then left.

The Basha and Rachael situation is now on the news. They have been arrested in connection with the burglary along with a third person, a cousin of Basha's. They still haven't recovered my mother's saltwater pearl necklace. Part of me is glad they got caught, but it's sad what lengths Basha and Rachael went to. Basha is a woman scorned. After months of discussions with Uncle Frenchy, Caleb, and Cassandra, Aunt Mary has made the decision to adopt Rosie. When I was volunteering at Aunt Mary's youth center this summer, Rosie always mentioned she wanted Aunt Mary to adopt her. We were all moved to tears, especially when Rosie presented Aunt Mary with a drawing of a girl whose heart had been mended back together.

James has finally apologized for making me feel that I wasn't worthy of JB. He also said how sorry he was for suggesting I terminate my pregnancy. He has fallen in love with Melody. He and Judy even take her for walks in the neighborhood. I'm glad things are finally looking up for us.

\*\*\*

I'm sitting next to JB, holding his hand inside Madison Square Garden. Joining us at the table are his parents, his agent, his coach, Caleb, Paul, and Jake. Anna is here too. I'm telling myself to trust

JB around her—believe him when he says everything with them is strictly professional. One night we were lying in bed talking, and her name came up in the conversation. I notice with JB he lives by the credo, *Your feelings might get hurt, but if you want the truth, all you do is ask.* I asked how many times he slept with Anna, he said twice. First time happened the night they met and last year when she was in a celebratory mood following her divorce. He tells me women approach him all the time, and although they may catch his eye, they will never have his heart. I remember Gilda's words to me, "Maddie, don't be a fool."

The commissioner approaches the podium and reads the name of the number one draft pick. The cheers of the fans are deafening, and all the people at his table are cheering and celebrating him. The player walks up to stand with the team officials holding the jersey. I sit a little on edge, feeling JB squeeze and hold my hand as each player after him is called, and they go through the formalities of shaking hands and holding the jersey with their name and number on it. Then the commissioner announces JB's name and the team that drafts him is from New Jersey. While the deafening cheers of the fans ring throughout the arena, JB turns to me, and we kiss. He stands and gives James a handshake and a hug. He gives Judy a hug, as well as his coach. JB, dressed in a gray double-breast power suit, walks with a cool gait to the podium where he dons a hat and holds up the jersey with his name and number. Judy wipes away tears, moving in the empty seat where JB sat to give me a hug.

It's late in the evening when JB and I get back to the hotel suite. Gilda has Melody in her arms, and I am surprised Melody's still awake. My breasts are full, but right now I'm too excited to pump.

"Congratulations," Gilda says to JB.

"Thank you," he says, before leaning in to give Melody a kiss. "We did it, baby."

Melody's alert. She smiles and coos at the sound of JB's voice.

"If you two need to finish celebrating, Melody and I will be in the room down the hall. You still have enough breast milk stored, so don't worry."

"Thank you, Gilda." I give her a big, warm hug before she walks down the hall with Melody.

JB and I enter our bedroom suite, closing the door behind us we both do a celebration dance around the room. I'm flinging my hair, jumping up and down while he's doing the robot.

"We did it," he says.

"Yes, we did."

"You got into Juilliard. I'm in the pros."

"I'm so happy."

"Guest what. The offer is good too," he says. "Right now, my agent is negotiating as we speak. We're looking at $2.1 million guaranteed for four years."

"That's wonderful."

"I'm buying you a bigger ring," he says.

"There's nothing wrong with this. I love it."

"You do?"

"Of course," I say, looking at my quarter carat diamond ring he purchased for three hundred bucks from a pawn shop on Crenshaw.

"That's why I love you," he says, kissing me. "You only want me. I feel it, Maddie."

"I'm so glad this all worked out. I'm at Juilliard. You're playing with a team in New Jersey."

"I'm getting us a house in New Jersey with enough room for an indoor basketball court, a music studio and a huge back yard."

"I can't wait, I'm so excited." I'm gushing.

Then I notice his expression change from upbeat to serious.

"What?"

"I'm still waiting on a response from the IOC."

"Don't worry, those Olympic people will call and you will go to South Korea and represent team USA."

That seem to bring a smile upon his lips. We kiss and hold each other. It's been a long time, but I can truly say right now I am filled with joy.

# About the Author

T. Wendy Williams is a native of Huntsville, Texas and a 1996 graduate of Sam Houston State University. A Melody for Madeline is Williams' fourth novel. She is also author of Lost in the Music, Mile High Confessions, and Happily Never After. Her novels have been featured in Essence magazine, the New York Review of Books and Black Authors Matter TV. Williams is proud wife to husband, Joseph, and loving mother to their children, Layla, Miles, and Lance. Currently, Williams resides in Suburban Houston where she is writing her fifth book.

Connect with T. Wendy online:

Instagram @twendywilliams

Twitter @twendytheauthor

Facebook @twendywilliams

Website: www.twendytheauthor.com

# Acknowledgments

I give thanks to Almighty God. A special thank you to my husband, Joseph, and our three children: Layla, Miles, and Lance. Thank you to my parents, my mother, Bobbie, and my father, Terry. Thank you to my editor, Chandra Sparks Splond, you are truly amazing. Thank you, Renee Taplin Jones for being available to answer my questions. Thank you, Janice Harding for supporting me and getting all your girlfriends to read my books. Thank you to Gwen Richardson and Dr. Rhonda Lawson with Black Authors Matter TV for all your support and getting the public aware of my works with your amazing platform. Last but not least, thank you readers for your outpouring love.